I0538201

VELCRO
THE NINJA KAT

CHRIS WIDDOP

I would like to thank Uncle Bob, Aunt Laurie, and Rachel Rice, whose critical enthusiasm and words of wisdom helped guide this book down the right path. Thank you to Derrick Buxton and Dao Lam, who never stopped believing in me and constantly kept pushing me along the way. To Natalia Locatelli, who was always there to lend a helping hand during the publishing process. To my artist and resident fangirl, Sharon Kemmerer, and to all of my friends who helped out in any way. But most importantly, I need to say thanks to my family. Mom, Dad, Valita, Adam, Tim, John, Jason, Billy, this couldn't be possible without all of you in my life.

Chapter 1

'What is the meaning of this?'

That was the thought running through the minds of the citizens of Highland. Just on the outskirts of the village were two active soldiers of their own country's military, the Devil Corps. The two feline Devils were unconscious and tied up to wooden posts, their butts planted firmly on the grass. As the various animals of the village looked on in awe, a pair of towering black bulls, members of Highland's armored guard unit, accompanied a medic cat through the crowd to tend to the Devils. .

"Man," said Rocky, a short, slender gray tabby cat, whose words flew out in a jittery rush. "Who would do such a thing to our own military, huh, Stan?"

"Maybe it was that terrorist," said Stan, his voice surprisingly high pitched. He was a large, pudgy cat whose fur formed a pattern of black and white patches like a cow.

"Huh? Terrorist?" said Rocky. "What terrorist?"

"You know, that rogue ninja," said Stan. "The guy who's supposedly attacking the Devil Corps head on. *The Ninja Kat.*"

"Huh, now that you mention it, Stan, I *have* heard about this same sorta thing happening at other villages, Stan."

"But why would this Ninja Kat be doing such a thing?" Stan asked. "Do you think our country's under attack?"

"I'm dunno, Stan. But from what I hear, the Ninja Kat might actually be the one *preventing* an attack, Stan."

"Hey now, just what are you getting at?"

"What I'm saying is, what if it's not the Ninja Kat who's attacking *us*? What if it's really the *Devil Corps* who're trying to attack us, and the Ninja Kat is actually *saving* all of these villages."

"What? Impossible!" Stan said. "How could you even think such a thing of our own military? What possible reason could they have to attack their own people?"

As the conversation became heated, one cat managed to keep his cool. Looking out through his slick shades, the black tabby, Charlie, stood tall in his leather jacket and dark blue jeans, observing the laid out Devils with an eager smile spread across his scarred face.

"Boys," Charlie intervened, wrapping his arms around Rocky's and Stan's necks. "How about tonight, we meet this Ninja Kat for ourselves."

The eyes of the two younger cats widened in unison.

"W-what? Are you s-serious?" Stan said.

"Yeah, Charlie," Rocky said. "What if I'm wrong, Charlie? What if Stan's right? What if the Ninja Kat really *is* a terrorist, Charlie?"

"Well that's exactly what we're going to find out. Tonight, we'll settle the matter and put all the rumors to rest." Charlie smiled, showing off his sharp fangs. "After we've finished having *fun* with this Ninja Kat, of course."

Charlie placed his hands on his hips, looking over in eager anticipation at the fallen Devils being attended to. His two subordinates, on the other hand, turned to one another and shared a worried gulp.

Later that night, Charlie watched from the brush as Stan and Rocky, garbed in the borrowed camouflage uniforms of the laid out Devils, set out into the deep, dark forest outside their village. They traveled along a path that would lead them to the nearest neighboring village, hoping to lure out the Ninja Kat in the process. They tried their hardest to advance in a believable military manner, avoiding the crunching leaves with soft steps and brushing carefully past low limbs. Silently they moved, until the snap of a twig under Rocky's foot brought that silence to an abrupt end.

"Rocky!" Stan hissed, twirling around to scold his partner.

"Uh, whoops! My bad. Sorry. Promise it won't happen again-"

"Shh!" Stan said, bringing a finger to his mouth. "Now come on, let's just keep moving along."

The rambunctious Rocky agreed, springing to a salute with a new sense of motivation. "Right! Yes sir! Won't happen again. Let's keep moving. Right!" Stan rolled his eyes as he turned back around, and the two continued on their march.

And then another twig snapped.

"*Rocky!*"

"It wasn't me this time," Rocky said, looking behind himself. "I don't see anything, Stan. What do you think, Stan? You think it's him, Stan? Stan?" Rocky waited for a response, but it never came. "Stan?" Rocky turned to face the spot where his larger friend was standing only moments before. But all that he found was the darkness of the forest that surrounded him.

"... Stan?" Rocky whimpered. And now, all alone in

the black, haunting forest, the frightened cat began to shake in his false fatigues.

Then Charlie heard a rustling sound coming from just ahead. "Rocky, get down!" Charlie sprang out of the bushes. Rocky immediately heeded his leader's orders, dropping down face first as Charlie flew right over him. Charlie revealed his razor sharp claws, and as he passed by his approaching perpetrator, he swatted his paw. His claws hit their mark, and Charlie purred as he felt his victim's blood seep into his fur.

As he landed, Charlie whipped his crooked tail, eagerly awaiting the first sight of the supposed terrorist. The cat who stood before him wore a tight black outfit that covered every inch of his body, and carried a sword on his back. He was sleek, fit, and similar in size to Charlie. The menacing cat turned around quickly, revealing his black mask, a silhouette of his feline head.

In a dark outline sewn on the face of the cat's mask were two large, piercing eyes. There was hate, anger in those eyes. But most of all, Charlie saw determination in those eyes. He saw the drive to fight for what you believe in, and to succeed in that fight at all costs. Charlie was very familiar with those eyes. He saw them every day when he looked in the mirror.

"Heh, so you're the Ninja Kat, eh?" Charlie smirked.

The Ninja Kat said nothing. He merely observed his new challenger.

"What's the matter, kitty cat?" Charlie asked after the cat neglected to respond. He showingly lifted his blood stained hand. "Didn't get your tongue, too, did I?"

As the pain of the earlier strike settled in, the Ninja Kat clutched his bleeding stomach.

"Heh, you're not so tough," Charlie said, crouching

for his next attack.

The Ninja Kat furrowed his brows. He reached back and grabbed the hilt of his sword.

"Yeah, I figured you'd prob'ly be packin'," Charlie said, reaching behind his own back. "And so I came prepared." Charlie unsheathed his own sword, then awaited the Ninja Kat's next move.

He didn't expect what happened next, though. The black ninja calmed himself and snapped his sword back into place. "Huh? What the...?" Charlie was perplexed. It appeared that his challenger was preparing to retreat. "Grr-you're not getting away!"

Charlie charged, slashing away with his sword, but the Ninja Kat leapt backwards, dodging Charlie's every swipe. This infuriated the black tabby, who slashed out with increasing ferocity. The Ninja Kat hopped up, placing his feet against a tree behind him. Charlie reared back his sword, but as he thrust it forward, the Kat sprang up and over Charlie's head.

Charlie was forced to watch as the blade of his sword lodged deeply into the tree's trunk. The frustrated cat muttered under his breath as he tugged at it. "Gahrrr, stupid thing." By the time he finally managed to pull it out, though, it was too late.

The Ninja Kat had fled the scene.

After a few silent moments had passed, Rocky slowly got back to his feet. "W-what happened, Charlie?"

Charlie ignored the young cat, looking down at his claws, at the blood that stained them. He took in a whiff, then his paw began to shake, and he clenched his fist tight.

"Charlie?"

"Grr-you can't run away forever!" Charlie screamed into the night. "You *scaredy cat*! You can't just run away from

me! Do you hear me?! Huh?! I said do you hear me?! You...
idiot!" Charlie's entire body began to shake uncontrollably.

"H-hey," Rocky said. "S-so what do you t-think
happened to S-Stan?" As he said that, a faint, muffled cry
could be heard in the distance. "Hey, do you hear that,
Charlie?" Rocky asked, following after the sound, "I think it
might be Stan, Charlie."

But Charlie couldn't be bothered with such a concern
at the moment. He only continued to stand by, growling with
every breath he took.

In his mad dash, the Ninja Kat swiftly rushed
through the forest, successfully fleeing the scene. As he ran,
he could no longer ignore the pain of his wound as he had
during his brief scuffle with Charlie. And so, with a grunt, he
placed his palm over his bleeding stomach.

'*That guy,*' the Ninja Kat hissed to himself. '*Just what
was he trying to prove, luring me out like that? Tch!*' The Kat
smacked his face with his free palm, dropping his head. '*I
can't believe I fell for such an obvious trap.*'

'*Still,*' the Ninja Kat continued in thought, seriousness
returning in his tone. '*Was he really that desperate for a
challenge? Or maybe he was trying to capture me. Is it possible that
he was actually trying to do something noble for once? After all, I
do have that reputation following me around. If only they all knew
the truth...*'

The black ninja quickly shook his head, finding it
impossible to believe his own thoughts. '*No, that can't be it.
That's not Charlie. I know him. I know that look he had. He was
definitely just out looking for another fight. That idiot.*'

The Ninja Kat let out a sigh. '*So reckless, he hasn't
grown up at all. It looks like I still can't count on him after all. It's
too bad, too. He's a hell of a fighter.*' He looked down at his

stomach, pulling his hand away just slightly to see his bloody injury for himself. *'Only him. I can't believe I still let him catch me off guar-'*

The Ninja Kat's eyes sprang open under his mask. And with a quick, decisive sting to the back of his neck, the Ninja Kat blacked out.

Chapter 2

The Ninja Kat woke up in a groggy state. His vision still fuzzy, he looked around, curious as to his current whereabouts. *'Whe... where am I?'* As his vision gradually improved, he found that he was within a round, wooden room. The walls, the floor, everything in the well lit room appeared to be made of wood.

As he sat up in his bed, he rubbed his head, still a bit woozy, and he noticed an odd buzzing sound. He looked up towards this strange noise and stared in awe. The entire ceiling was swarming with bees, buzzing about and hard at work.

The Kat didn't have too long to gawk, though, as the door to his room opened. "Ah, so you've awakened!" The Kat looked over curiously and saw as he was joined by, of all things, four hamsters who walked into the room. "Good, good," continued the elderly hamster in the lead of the group. This hamster stood about waist-high to the cat, holding himself up with a wooden cane. He sported a large white, fluffy mustache which covered his mouth, though his delighted expression remained quite visible.

"Where am I?" the Ninja Kat demanded, his voice soft, yet threatening. "And... how did you bring me here?"

"Ah yes, well, lets see," the elder hamster began. He

cleared his throat, then began his introductions. "My name is Huck. And I am the Elder Ham. And, as I see you've noticed, up above are the bees." The elder turned his attention once more to the ceiling above, looking up with thankful eyes. "They have allowed us to stay within their houses during these trying times. These days, we live with them, within the trees, though that has not always been the case."

As he spoke, one particular bee pulled himself away from the swarm, flying down to the Ninja Kat's bed. "Ah, and this little one is Buzzbee. You asked how we brought you here. Well, it was actually this bee who stung you before. And it must have been quite a sting at that, you've been out for quite a whi..."

Huck's words came to a screeching halt, as he and his fellow hamsters watched on in bewilderment at the sight of the Ninja Kat playfully batting out at the buzzing Buzzbee. The Kat looked ridiculous, acting like a kitten while garbed in his dark, frightening mask and uniform.

Noticing the silence, the Kat suddenly became aware of his silly situation and immediately put an end to it. Buzzbee quickly made his getaway, rejoining his fellow bees up above. The Kat, meanwhile, regained his composure, trying his best to play it off as if nothing had happened. Still, he couldn't help but feel embarrassed.

"Ah, hmm..." Huck continued awkwardly. "Ah yes. As I was saying. We haven't always lived here among the bees. No, it wasn't long ago that we lived prosperously within the confines of our own village, Smartland."

The hamster let out a sigh at the mention of his village. "Ah, Smartland. It was a busy village, and a happy one. And it was a village in constant evolution. Our people were always conjuring up new ideas..."

The Kat could see vividly the images of the hamster's

village as the Elder Ham proceeded to describe it. He saw the city streets, so alive, with tall buildings where the hamsters worked hard on their constantly advancing technology. The long, colorful tubes, filled with hamsters as they made their way through the city, protruding from building to building, and wrapping all around the city. The busy streets that were packed with large, vibrant ball-like vehicles. And he could see the peaceful neighborhoods, lined up with rectangular houses, where the hamsters lived their happy, carefree lives.

These memories brought a smile to Huck's face, though his smile never managed to stick around for too long as his thoughts lingered on. "These are indeed trying times, though I'm certain that you're well aware of that already." As the tone in Huck's voice veered, the Ninja Kat listened intently. "We know all about this secret war that the Devil Corps is waging on our villages in the Widow Country. We know this, because we were victims of this war.

"Not too long ago, our village was targeted by the Devils. And their attack was flawless." Huck's mustache ruffled. "They entered the village completely undetected. Then once inside, one by one, they proceeded to demolish the buildings within our city.

"It became an easy battleground for them in the confusion and panic that resulted from this destruction. As we tried in vain to run away, more buildings were toppled, and more casualties followed. It soon became apparent that there were no safe places to run to within the village, and so, seeing no other alternative, our people fought.

"We hamsters are not known for our expertise in combat, but that didn't stop us from trying. However, our people found this fight to be unlike any other that we could possibly even imagine. The Devils, they fought us off using an... *eerie* power. This power, it made the Devils strong,

10

stronger than any Devil I've ever seen before. This power, it was dark, sinister. We weren't prepared for something like this. Despite all our advanced defenses, we were no match for this dark power.

"It wasn't long before the Devils had taken the village. Once the fighting had ended, they offered the survivors of this massacre a chance to join them. But when no one stepped forward, they continued their slaughter. Finally, the remaining hamsters had had enough, and they resisted no more. They were taken prisoner, and marched out of the village.

"And as this was happening, all we could do was watch." Huck lowered his head in shame. "I saved as many hamsters as I could. We managed to escape into the forest. There, hidden away in the trees, we watched helplessly as the rest of our people were left to hopelessly fend for themselves." Huck shook his head, letting out a deep sigh of sorrow.

"We've since formed an alliance with the bees of the forest. Baring witness to the mayhem themselves, they understood our position, and, graciously, they allowed us to reside within their hollowed trees.

"They have since kept us informed on the fate of the hamsters taken prisoner. Being much more capable of sneaking about unnoticed, the bees have kept a watchful eye on our friends. They are being held prisoner within a military prison not too far from here, a brig known as The Web."

The Ninja Kat nodded. "Yes, I'm familiar with that place."

"Ah, I had a feeling you might be," Huck responded. "And that's exactly why we brought you here. You have been fighting this war much longer than we have, and our village has become a casualty. We share a common goal. We want to see an end to this war before any more villages have to suffer the same fate as we.

"I also assume that you have a great deal of intel on our enemy," Huck continued. "After all, how else could it be that you've been able to locate and prevent so many similar situations from taking place?" The Ninja Kat was a little annoyed by the Elder Ham's insinuations, but kept his mouth shut nonetheless. "That intel could prove to be very handy in our resistance."

The Kat stared intently at Huck. "And just what is it, exactly, that you intend to do?"

"Ah, well first, we intend to free the hamsters held prisoner within The Web, and any other prisoners of war who may be held captive there. And we were hoping that you would aid us in this rescue mission. With the skills that you've shown, and your admitted familiarity with this prison, you would be a valuable asset in this mission.

"We're not asking you to do this alone, mind you. Behind me is my hand picked squad who I intend to send along with you." Huck stepped aside, allowing the three hamsters behind him to take center stage. He pointed out to the first hamster in line, a dwarf hamster who, unlike his light brown friends, wore a gray coat of fur. "This is Buttons."

"Howdy there," Buttons said, bringing two fingers up towards the distinct black stripe on his forehead in a saluting gesture.

"He is one of our smartest hamsters, and, since the attack, has been working diligently on a defense to the dark power I had alluded to before.

"And next is Chippy," Huck said, pointing to the big hamster who stood in the middle of the trio. "He's as strong as he looks, and extremely loyal to his friends. He should prove to be of great assistance should you find yourself in a tough spot." He was by far the largest hamster that the Ninja Kat had ever seen. He towered over his peers, and was probably even taller than the Kat himself. Though he was big, and he appeared to be tough, there was a look of innocence that stayed ever present on his face as he smiled at the Kat.

"And finally, Flash." The third hamster was young and scruffy, and stood at a similar height as his elder. "This mission probably means more to him than anyone else. In fact, he actually *insisted* on being a part of this mission."

Flash had a bitter look on his face. His head lay low, and not once did he lift his eyes. "Come on now, Flash," Huck said, "don't be shy. Say hello to our guest." Flash lifted his eyes in the Kat's direction, but then quickly pulled them away again. He opened his mouth to say something, but all that came out was a grumble under his breath. Huck let out a sigh at the hamster's reaction, but said no more on the matter.

The Kat placed his hands on his knees, taking in all that he had heard and looked down as he prepared to put it to thought. As he looked down, though, he remembered his wounds that he had suffered earlier. They had been treated. The Kat patted at his stomach, and sure enough, he had been patched up.

"Ah, yes, you were quite a mess when we brought you in, so we took it upon ourselves to treat your injury." As the Kat rubbed his stomach, he realized that his bandages remained hidden underneath his black outfit. And if that were the case, then that meant...

"Don't worry," Huck insisted, quickly responding to the deadly look that the Ninja Kat had shot in his direction. "I assure you, your secret will remain safe with us." The Ninja Kat let out a huff in annoyance, but found he had no choice but to place his trust in the hamsters.

"Now then, lets move along now," Huck spoke to his

13

squad of hamsters, leading them out of the room. "Lets give our guest some space." The hamsters filed out, one after the other.

As Flash made his way out, he paused at the door. His back turned to the Kat, he lifted his head and looked over his shoulder. For a brief moment, his eyes met the Kat's. And though they exchanged glances for only a moment, the pain in Flash's eyes made it feel like an eternity had passed. But Flash was quick to pull his eyes away, and he stormed out of the room.

"Now then," Huck started, "get some rest, and I hope that you'll give some serious thought to all that I've said." The Kat nodded, and just like that, he was left alone to his thoughts.

Placing his hands on his knees once more, the Ninja Kat pondered deeply on all that he had just learned. *'I couldn't save these hamsters. I can't believe I wasn't there to protect them. If this was able to happen without my knowing, I wonder, what else have I missed? Who else has been a victim that I don't know about?'*

He clenched tightly at the cloth of his black uniform. *'I can only prevent so many attacks from happening, but in the end, it's only a delaying tactic. If I just keep doing what I've been doing, another incident is certain to happen. I can't allow that! It's time to take this fight to the next step. The time for action is now!'*

The Kat felt a surge of motivation rush through his body. *'Since this has happened, word is surely bound to spread. Soon, the Widow Country will learn of the war that the Devil Corps has secretly waged against them. And then they'll realize what it is that I've been doing this whole time. This will change everything. The people will know. And they'll fight. And then...'* the Ninja Kat then came to a horrible realization. The thoughts of an all out war against the military were too much to handle, and he quickly shook them from his head. *'No, it'd be a massacre. I can't let that happen.*

'But I also can't allow something like this happen again, either. I won't let anyone else die. I'll see to it that no one else has to suffer. I'll put an end to this war myself.

'And then,' the Ninja Kat continued, as the image of a *particular* Devil appeared in his mind. A large musclebound canine, whose vicious eyes gleamed, and whose menacing grin haunted the Kat's thoughts. *'Then, I'll have my revenge.'*

While the Kat seethed in anger, an unexpected knock at the door snapped him out of his vengeful daze. The Kat turned his attention to the door and was taken aback as his visitor stepped in.

"You..."

Chapter 3

The next day, the hamsters all gathered around in another large, round room that stood at the end of a long hallway. This room was a much quieter one without any bees buzzing above. Here they waited patiently for their guest's response, the three younger hamsters sitting on a large couch while the elder insisted upon leaning against his cane.

As the Ninja Kat stepped out of his room, the three hamsters stood to their feet. Huck looked up at the cat and cheerily greeted him. "Ah, good morning!"

The Kat wasted no time rushing towards the round table that stood in the center of the room.

"Ah, where are my manners," Huck continued. "Can I get you anything? Something to eat perhaps? Or-"

BAM!

The cat slammed his palms down on the table, cutting the Elder Ham short. The Kat looked forward, staring out at Huck with his menacing eyes. "Here's the plan." The Ninja Kat looked over the squad of hamsters within the room. "I'm assuming that this is all who'll be taking part in this mission. In that case, it would be best to tackle this thing from two fronts."

The Kat shot a finger in Button's direction. "You. You and the big one here," he said, referring to Chippy, "you two

16

will be pairing up."

The cat then looked over at Flash. As he did, Flash's eyes instinctively shifted away. "And as for you," the Kat began, "you'll be teaming up with me." Flash slowly returned his gaze to the black ninja, the scruffy hamster looking at him curiously.

"Ah, well I'm certainly happy to hear that you're willing to help us," Huck said, impressed. "And it appears that you've already put a lot of thought into our plan of attack. That's just like you, always staying a step ahead of us. It's no wonder it took Buzzbee so long to track you down."

The Kat looked down, patting at his bandaged stomach. "You healed my wounds. You helped me, and now I owe you. So yes, I'll help you on this mission..." The Kat paused, pondering his next words. He looked up at the hamsters before him, his eyes ultimately landing on Flash. This time though, Flash didn't pull his eyes away.

The Kat focused on the pain in Flash's eyes, a pain so strong that, even in the hamster's amazement, it ceased to fade away. The cat's thoughts from the night before still fresh in his mind, he silently swore to never allow anyone to experience such pain again.

"After this mission, though," the Kat finally continued, snapping his gaze over to Huck, "you will all stay out of my way." Huck looked bewildered by the Kat's remarks, but the Kat continued before Huck could utter a single word of objection. "You said that the Devils had used some sort of dark power against you. Tell me what you know of it."

"Ah, yes of course. I'm not entirely sure as to what it was that they used, though I do have my, ah, '*theories*' as to what it might be." Huck's tone became more cautious as he spoke. "As for what I witnessed, as I mentioned last night,

17

this power, whatever it was, it appeared to make its casters exceptionally strong. It consumed these Devils, surrounding them with some sort of dark aura. As relentless as the soldiers were before, with this power, they became that much more menacing, that much more frightening!

"But a mere increase in their physical strength wasn't the full extent of this power," the elder continued. "That aura, they were able to shape it, to use it as a weapon itself. And as I said, none of our defenses were good against it. As it made contact with our shields, the dark substance instantly spread, consuming them like it had its casters. But unlike the Devils, it rotted our shields, like some sort of plague."

"You said that you've been working on a defense to this power," the Ninja Kat stated.

"Ah yes," Huck said, turning to the short gray hamster to his side. "Buttons-"

"Yeah, I been workin' somethin' up," Buttons began, speaking in a thick southern accent. He turned around, heading towards the large hallway behind him. "You see, none of our de-fenses worked against that dark stuff before, so it didn't make much sense to build the same ol' thing, you know?" His voice began to trail off as he continued down the hall, turning a corner.

"So I asks the Elder Ham what he thinks the stuff is, right?!" The hamster continued, now well out of sight and yelling. "Well, turns out he has an idea or two of what it might be! So seein' as that's all I got to work with, I ain't got much choice but to build our new de-fense on an ol' theory, you know?!"

The Ninja Kat looked on, wondering just where this little hamster had run off to. He didn't have to wait long for an answer, though, as Buttons made his way back around the corner in the most curious way. He rolled back into view, riding inside of a large, ball-like vehicle, within which Buttons could clearly be seen.

"So here it is," Buttons said proudly, rejoining his teammates. "Whatcha think?"

'*I am* not *riding in that,*' the Ninja Kat thought bluntly.

Buttons humphed at the Kat's lack of a reaction. "Didn't think you'd appreciate it. Don't you worry though, I'm not expectin' ya to be rollin' around in one of these." With that, he pressed a button which popped four rectangular fragments off of the sides of his ball. "That's why I made these here shields."

Buttons stepped out of his ball, grabbing the four clear shields which he handed out to his teammates. "Figured they'd be more practical than rollin' around the prison like such. They're made of, er, '*all na-tu-ral*' stuff. Figurin' that the Elder Ham's theory is right, these should work against this dark stuff we're up against."

The Ninja Kat held his piece of the little hamster's ball up in front of him, observing it. "You keep mentioning this 'theory' of the Elder Ham's." The Kat pulled his eyes away from the shield, looking dead ahead at Huck. "Just what exactly is this theory?"

"Ah, uh, hmm," Huck nervously stumbled on his words, looking around the room as if searching for an answer to the Kat's question.

"Who wants some cookies?"

Everyone shot their heads in the direction of the hallway, where a new hamster was standing. She was an elderly female ham, dressed in a flowery apron and holding a tray of freshly baked cookies in her oven gloved hands. She wore a huge smile on her face as she happily greeted the group.

"Ah, yes, Thomasina!" Huck spoke with relief in his

voice as he rushed over to the elderly woman's side. Chippy managed to beat the elder to the woman, though, and he intended on helping himself to the chewy treats. "Yes, we're quite busy here, as you can see," Huck stated, shooing the larger hamster out of the way. "We'd certainly enjoy some of your cookies later on, though." Chippy was visibly disappointed by the elder's comment. "Come now, lets not interrupt the mission planning, hmm?"

Huck turned Thomasina around, placing his arm over her shoulder as he lead her down the hallway and out of the room. Huck clearly couldn't leave the room quick enough. The Ninja Kat was quite perplexed by the elder's strange actions, and couldn't help but wonder just what it was that the hamster had to hide.

* * *

With their shields strapped to their backs, the group made their way through the nighttime forest, heading towards The Web. They were led by Buzzbee, who was most familiar with the rout. In the rear, Chippy pulled out a sack. His mouth watering, he reached in and pulled out a handful of delicious cookies, stuffing his face with the chewy treats. Buttons looked over curiously in the direction of the chewing sound, and his jaw dropped in shock and disbelief.

"Ahh! Chippy! What in blazes do ya think you're doin'?!" Chippy's eyes saddened, and for a moment he ceased to chew on his snack. "You see, this is why you're so dern big, ya know. Because ya can't go a dern minute without stuffin' your face with somethin'." As the dwarf hamster berated him, Chippy sunk his head. "And on a mission! Do ya see what you're doin' there!" Buttons yelled, pointing down at the crumbs on the ground. "You're leavin' a trail for the enemy to follow us back."

"And with your yelling," the Ninja Kat hissed, snapping around to the yapping ham, "you're informing the enemy of our current location!"

Buttons zipped his mouth shut, and the Ninja Kat sighed under his mask. '*Maybe it wasn't such a good idea to pair those two up.*' The Kat glanced back, observing the large hamster whose cheeks were still filled with cookies, and the dwarf hamster who continued to look irritated. '*Then again, I'm not so sure I'd be able to put up with either of them myself.*'

Shaking his head, the Kat returned to more important matters, "The Elder Ham acted strange when I asked him to explain his theory."

"Er, well," Buttons began, looking away awkwardly and rubbing the back of his head. "Wwee're not exactly supposed to talk about it-"

"I'll tell you." All heads looked over to Flash.

"Flash, no!" Buttons objected.

"No, Buttons," Flash said, keeping his eyes locked ahead of him as he spoke. "He needs to know." The Kat listened attentively. "The Elder Ham thinks that the dark power is something that's supposed to be long extinct. Something known as Black Magic."

Buttons sighed, then continued on with Flash's explanation. "I designed these here shields with Black Magic in mind. Like I said, it's all we had to go on. But the Elder Ham still didn't want us to go into this thing with only one idea in mind, since it may not even *be* Black Magic. After all, the stuff ain't supposed to exist anymore."

"If that's all we have to go on, though," the Kat inquired, "wouldn't it have made sense to bring it up while we were planning?"

"Probably," Buttons answered, "but... it's just, well,

talk of this Black Magic stuff is supposed to be strictly pro-
hibited, and the Elder's still sorta stuck in those ways-"

"It's that mindset that's got us here right now!" Flash
butted in. "If we had known what we were up against, if we
were able to prepare for it, then we might not have lost
everything. And if we continue thinking like those 'old ways',
then we're never going to stand a chance in this war!"

After Flash's frustrated outburst, the group remained
silent the rest of the way. As the Kat reflected upon the
hamster's passionate words, his mind trailed back to the night
prior.

He didn't have too long to reflect, however, as it
wasn't much longer before Buzzbee suddenly zipped
upwards, signaling the group to a halt. Cautiously, they
peered through the trees.

"We're here."

Chapter 4

The Ninja Kat made quick work sneaking the group through the razor sharp fencing that surrounded The Web. He pointed out the entry point that Buttons and Chippy would take, then, alongside Flash, he wasted no time traversing through the shadowy plains of the prison grounds towards his own destination.

Buttons and Chippy looked to one another and nodded, both hamsters trying their hardest to hide their worry behind masks of confidence. Then they turned their attention to the prison itself. It was a large, haunting brick structure with a lonely presence to it. As the hamsters cautiously made their approach, they noticed the lack of posted security guards and search lights. It was creepy, a feeling that made their hairs stand on end.

Their suspicious feeling was reinforced as the two entered the building with little effort. Pressing their backs to the wall, they looked around and found the place completely deserted. They stealthily made their way through the dimly lit halls of the prison. But the less signs of life that they found, the more complacent they gradually grew.

"Hey Chippy," Buttons finally whispered as they turned a corner. "Do ya maybe think we might've gone to the wrong place?"

Chippy didn't respond. Instead, the big ham stopped cold in his tracks. "Chippy?" Gulping, Buttons slowly turned to see what brought Chippy to such a sudden halt.

What he saw, standing before them, was a little brown lop-eared bunny rabbit. The rabbit stood on all fours, looking up at the two larger hamsters with its big, bulging eyes. For some time, the two parties stared at one another, neither budging an inch.

"Well, what do you think?" Buttons whispered to Chippy, never peeling his eyes away from the innocent looking rabbit. "He doesn't look like any Devil I've seen. Maybe he's friendly?" Chippy shrugged his shoulders in response. Buttons dipped down and slowly extended an arm to the small rabbit. "H-h-hey there..."

The rabbit twirled around, hopping away in a mad dash.

"Crap! C'mon, Chip," Buttons said, shooting up to his feet. "We can't let him get away!" The two hamsters made chase. They ran their fastest, yet struggled to keep up with the rabbit. The rabbit zipped around a corner, and when the hamsters reached the same corner, the rabbit was already on the far end of the next hall. "Dammit, Chip, this ain't gonna cut it!" Buttons pushed forward, leaving his friend in the dust. When he made it to the next hallway, though, the rabbit was well out of sight.

Chippy skidded to a halt once he caught back up with his partner. The big ham plopped down to his knees and panted furiously.

'This ain't good,' Buttons thought. *'If there is anyone here, we can't let that rabbit let them know we're here!'* After a short pause, Buttons grabbed his shield and went right back at it. "Catch up when ya can, Chip. I'm gonna get this son of a gun right now!"

Buttons jumped in the air. He pressed a button on his shield, then rolled up into a ball. His shield expanded around him, encompassing Buttons within a miniature version of his ball-like vehicle. As it landed on the ground, it blasted forward, zooming down the hallways in rapid fashion. Before long, Buttons caught up with the rabbit.

The sight of the approaching ball startled the rabbit, who popped into the air before continuing his mad dash. As fast as he hopped, he was no longer able to put any distance between himself and the barreling ball behind him. He turned a quick corner, and then another, but Buttons stayed right on his tail. In a panic, the rabbit found himself running down a final corridor with nowhere else to go. Buttons cornered the rabbit at a dead end, rolling to a stop as his ball smoothly compressed back into its shield form.

The hamster put his shield away, then slowly approached the little rabbit. "Looks like the end of the road for you, huh?" Buttons spoke in a cocky tone, towering over the small bunny. "About dern time, too." The rabbit cowered down, shaking in fear.

Buttons felt confident as the dim light above shined down upon him. However, his confident feeling soon disappeared, as his eyes widened at the sight before him.

"What in the..."

The small rabbit began to grow. It transformed into a monstrous shape, and its shadow completely cast over the dwarf hamster.

Chippy finally managed to catch up, plopping his hands back down onto his knees in a pant. As he lifted his head, though, his expression grew just as horrified as Buttons'. The two stood stiff, staring up in terror at the monster that now stood before them.

Chapter 5

On the other side of the brig, the Ninja Kat and Flash found it just as easy to break in, just as lonely within. Despite this, the Kat never once let his guard down. He hid within the shadows at all times and ensured that Flash followed his example.

As they reached the hatch at the end of the corridor, they pressed their backs against the wall. The Kat carefully peered through the window out of the corner of his eye, making sure the coast was clear. Sure enough, like every hallway before it, there wasn't a soul in sight.

The Kat carefully opened the door, urging Flash to rush in. He followed after, closing the door behind him without a sound and disappearing back into the shadows.

Flash, however, stood just where he was, in plain sight under the dim light.

"Flash!" The Kat quietly hissed. "What are you doing? We have to stay hidden!" But the Kat's words fell on deaf ears. Flash stood there, frozen, like a statue. The Kat then noticed that they were no longer alone.

On the far side of the hallway stood an odd looking character. He resembled a hamster, just a bit shorter than Flash. But his arms were machine-like, and connected in the rear to a pack on his back. Extending from his hands were clean, razor sharp claws that spanned all the way to the floor. He wore a dark, robotic looking helmet, shaped to form his hamster features. Where his eyes should have been were two glowing red visors, which glared out threateningly.

The Kat tilted his head in confusion. He was certain the hall was empty before they entered. It didn't matter now, though. With Flash standing in plain sight, this new hamster definitely knew they were here.

'*Looks like I have no choice,*' the Kat sighed. "Flash, you take cover, I'll handle this!" The Kat ran past Flash, but the scruffy ham remained still. The Kat turned back to the hamster, frustrated by his continued lack of response. "Flash!"

Flash had tears in his eyes. His lower lip was quivering, trying to form a word, though his mumbling was impossible to decipher over his endless sniffling.

The Kat took one more look at their apparent opponent, who had yet to move an inch himself. He wondered what it could be about him that got Flash this shaken up.

And then it dawned on him. '*Could it be?*'

As the Kat stared down his enemy, he made an effort to listen closely to the word that Flash was trying so desperately to say. Once he was finally able to make out this word, his thoughts instantly returned to the previous night.

* * *

"You..."

The Ninja Kat sat up in his bed, staring over at Flash, who stood at the doorway of the rounded, wooden room. Flash tried to look the Kat in the eyes, but he instead looked down towards the floor.

27

"I, um..." the scruffy hamster began nervously. "I wanted to talk to you." The Kat offered no verbal response. He stared the hamster down with the cold, dark gaze that was etched on his mask. This made the hamster appear even more nervous, but he forced his words out anyway.

"The Elder Ham told you that I requested to be on this mission," Flash began. "I wanted to tell you why."

The Kat was all ears.

"I, um..." He shifted his eyes, as if looking around for where to begin. "I... have a little brother. After we lost our parents, I had to take care of him. It wasn't always easy, since I was still a kid myself. But there was no one else there for him. So it was up to me.

"On the day of the attack, I was running late for school. My brother was still in bed when I left the house. I told him to hurry up and get ready. He promised he would, so... I left without him.

"I should have waited. I should have walked him to school. Make sure he didn't slack off again. But I was in a hurry." Flash began to tear up, then he whispered under his breath, "What kind of an older brother am I?" He took a hard sniff and quickly wiped his arm over his eyes.

"I was in class when it all started. Once it was clear that we were under attack, they had us evacuate. I tried my hardest to find my brother in the crowd, but it was impossible. I *did* find one of his classmates. I asked him if my brother ever made it to class." Flash paused, and his jaw began to shake. "He didn't.

"All I wanted was to get home. But when I got there, I could see *them* through the window." Flash was snarling. Even as the hamster stared at the floor, the Kat could see the sheer hatred in his eyes. "*The Devils*. They were in my house!

"I wanted to go in there, stand up to those Devils and

save my brother. But my body wouldn't move. If the Elder Ham hadn't snatched me away when he did, the Devils would have surely seen me. And I... I..."

Flash clenched his fists tightly, his eyes squinted shut as tears streamed out. "I wasn't there for him. All I could do was stand there. And now..." Flash's eyelids slid open, and his gaze finally stuck with the Kat's. "Now they've got my *brother.*

"So that's why I have to go on this mission. I have to save my little brother."

Flash bit down on his lower lip. He turned his head up towards the buzzing ceiling, allowing his tears to drip down to his feet. "I know he's there, I just know he is." Flash sounded as if he were trying to convince himself. "He just can't be..."

He gulped, cutting himself short as he apparently realized that he was thinking out loud. He immediately pulled his eyes back to his side, away from the Kat's. "A-anyways, I wanted to tell you that before you made your decision. We really need your help." Flash turned his back, heading towards the door.

"Wait," the Kat finally spoke, stopping Flash at the doorway. "Tell me," he said, genuine care in his voice, "what's your brother's name?"

Flash looked over his shoulder. "His name?" he asked. "It's..."

* * *

"... Slash."

The Kat listened closely as Flash silently uttered his younger brother's name.

"What are you saying?" The Kat questioned. "Do you think that this is Slash?"

Flash took in a hard whiff. "He's got his scent. And-"

Without warning, the mecha-hamster charged forward. The Ninja Kat unsheathed his sword, but the hamster leapt right over him. He reared back his long, sharp claws, diving headfirst towards Flash.

"Flash!" The Ninja Kat yelled. "Move!"

But, much to the Kat's horror, Flash still wouldn't budge. He was frozen solid. All Flash could do was squeeze his eyes shut and wait for it all to be over.

Chapter 6

As Slash dove towards Flash, all Flash could do was squeeze his eyes shut. Looking on in horror, the Ninja Kat pounced forward, tackling down Flash.

Crack!

Slash's blades stabbed directly into the shield on the Kat's back. However, the Kat wasn't concerned with that at the moment. "What were you thinking, just standing there like that?!" The Kat scolded. "Are you *trying* to get us both killed?!"

As the Kat yelled, Slash continued to force down on his claws. It didn't take much effort for him to shatter the Kat's shield. The hamster reared back for a more fatal stab, but the Kat twirled around and kicked the hamster off of him.

'Tch, so much for these shields being of any use,' the Kat mockingly thought to himself.

The Kat stood up, taking a readying stance with his sword in hand. "Get your head in the game, Flash," the Kat spoke down to the hamster. "We didn't come here just to hand ourselves over to the Devils."

Flash shook his head wildly. "No, no no no no NO! You don't understand!" The hamster yelled. "Don't you get it? That's not a *Devil!* That's my *brother!* That's *Slash!* What do you expect me to do? I'm supposed to save him, not fight him!"

The Ninja Kat sighed. "I know it must be hard for you," he said, calm but firm, "but even if our enemy *is* who you say he is, he *isn't*! This hamster is *not* your brother!" He paused, lowering his voice. "Not anymore, at least."

Slash bolted forward once more, and the Kat's sword clashed with the ham's claws. The Kat fought offensively, but Slash blocked every strike with ease. Once Slash found his opening, he sliced out at the Kat's head. As the Kat ducked, Slash headbutted his opponent with his metal helmet. Startled, the Kat fell to the ground, grabbing at his forehead.

With the Kat down, Slash eyeballed his elder brother, who remained lying on the ground. Flash was trembling in fright, but Slash remained uncaring as he lifted his claws into the light. He turned them towards Flash, who in turn clenched his eyes.

Slash struck down at the helpless hamster. However, once more, he failed to hit his mark.

The Kat threw himself on top of Flash again. But this time, the Kat didn't have a shield to block the blades from sticking into his back.

Shaking all over, Flash slowly peeled his eyes open. The Ninja Kat stared back, and asked, "Have you seen enough? Or am I going to have to *die* before you finally see the truth?"

Flash was speechless. His jaw propped open in astonishment at the Kat's selfless sacrifice. As Slash pulled his blood drenched blades from the ninja's back, the Kat let out an agonizing meow. Slash flung the blood onto the wall, then reared back for the killing blow.

The Kat wasn't ready to die just yet, though. His sword in hand, the Kat popped back to his feet. He swung out furiously, fighting on pure adrenaline, ignoring the impossible pain surging through him.

"I know what you're going through, Flash," the Kat spoke as he fought, determination in his voice. "I know what it's like to lose someone important. We share a similar goal of vengeance, to get back at those who took our loved ones from us. To stop them before they do the same to anyone else.

"But if you just give up right now, when we're so close to reaching that goal, then it's all for nothing. You'll never get another shot at redemption. You'll never get another chance to put an end to those who did *this* to your brother!"

Slash pulled the Kat's sword down with one hand. With the other, he backhanded the Kat's jaw with all of his mechanical might, effectively putting an end to the Kat's speech.

As his head was tossed to the side, the Kat could hear nothing, see nothing but bright stars dancing all around him. His body went limp as he stumbled to the floor. Gradually, the stars fluttered away, though his world continued to spin as he looked up at the menacing hamster.

Although the Kat's ears were still ringing, he swore he could hear someone screaming. Woozily, he turned his head towards Flash, who was finally back on his feet. With tears streaming down his face in a fit of rage, Flash was yelling a blood curdling war cry.

Flash grabbed his shield off his back and tugged on a pull cord. The rectangular sides of his shield fell to the ground, while the circular center in his hand spun like a saw. In a fury, he charged towards Slash, who was more than ready for him.

The Kat watched on in a daze as the two hamsters swung their weapons at one another. He tried to remain conscious, but that last blow, on top of all of the blood he lost, was just too much. As his eyes rolled to the back of his head under his mask, he only managed to make out one sound from the hamsters' clash. It was Flash's words, soft and timid, as he spoke to his younger brother.

"I'm sorry."

Chapter 7

The Ninja Kat was still hazy when he regained consciousness. It took him a moment to remember where he was and what had just happened. He winced as he pulled himself up, the pain shooting through his back serving as an instant reminder of his fight, though certain aspects remained blurry.

And then he noticed the two hamsters lying down face first in front of him. '*No...*'

The Kat crawled over to Flash. As he rolled the scruffy ham over, he was met with a pool of blood on the floor. The hamster took a hit in his chest, and blood continued to pour out as the Kat held him in his arms.

"Flash!" The Kat desperately shook the lifeless hamster. "Flash! Come on, wake up!" Flash was still breathing, though just barely. The shaken Kat laid the ham back down and feverishly attempted to stop the bleeding.

'*What have I done?*' he thought. '*This wasn't supposed to happen. Not like this.*'

The Kat took his eyes off of Flash for a moment in order to observe the fallen Slash. As he looked upon the mechanized ham, Flash's words rang loudly in his head. "*I'm supposed save him, not fight him!*"

'*I can't believe I made him do that. If it were me, if I had to go face to face with* him, *would I really be able to do it?*'

Then something curious about Slash distracted the Kat from his thoughts. On the pack on Slash's back was a black orb. There was a dark, misty substance swirling around within, something that looked very much alive. '*Wait, is that-?*'

"Ngh!" Flash groaned, instantly grabbing The Kat's attention.

"Flash! Can you hear me?" The Kat said, applying pressure to Flash's wounds. Flash's face curled in pain as he forced an eye open, looking up to the black clad ninja.

"I... I'm sorry."

"What are you talking about?" The Kat questioned.

"D-don't worry about me. Leave me. Save the rest of them."

"Shut up! You don't know what you're saying. You're gonna be okay," the Kat insisted, though there was a hint of doubt in his voice. "I'm not leaving you here like this."

As the Kat tried to convince his fallen friend that everything was going to be okay, the sounds of someone approaching threatened otherwise. The stomping of feet could be heard, heading from the direction the would-be rescuers had come. They couldn't be more than a few doors away, and they were approaching quickly.

The Kat looked down at the hamster in a panic. "Please," Flash pleaded, tugging on the Kat's sleeve, "I'm only going to hold you back."

The Ninja Kat was shaking his head. Conflicting thoughts were racing through his mind. As the footsteps drew closer, the Kat started acting instinctively. He pulled Flash up to his feet and wrapped Flash's arm over his shoulder. He tried to walk him away, but Flash pushed the Kat off.

"God dammit, Flash! We don't have time for this!"

"'We didn't come here just to hand ourselves over to the Devils.'" Flash quoted the Kat, falling down onto his hands and knees in the process.

"Flash..."

"That's what you said. You also said that we'll never get another shot if we get caught. I already failed my mission," Flash said, looking back at Slash. "But you've still got a chance to save the rest, before they do to them what they did to my *brother.*"

The door in the next hall over slammed open. They were almost out of time. "Please," Flash said, his arms trembling. His hands slipped on his blood, and his face rammed right into the floor. "Agh!" he screamed in pain. "GO!"

The Ninja Kat could only look away. Without another word, the Kat twirled around and made his way through the hatch to the next hallway. Hunched over, the Kat ran as fast as his wounded body would allow.

As he raced down the halls, his mind, too, was racing. This regret, leaving a comrade behind, struck him sharper than any blade ever could. His earlier regrets felt like a bee sting in comparison.

'I wasn't there to save the hamster's village,' he reflected. *'And now, even when I was there, I couldn't save Flash...'*

It took all of the Kat's willpower to force those negative thoughts out of his head. *'No! I can't think like that right now. I've got to stay focused. The rest of those hamsters are being held prisoner here somewhere. I'll never be able to save them in this frame of mind.'*

He looked back, listening for the sounds of his oncomers, but he couldn't hear them approaching any longer. *'They must have stopped when they saw those two. Flash, I swear*

I'll make this up to you.'

Distracted, the Kat was less than prepared when his feet failed to meet the ground. "What the...?" It was too late, he had already fallen into the hole in the floor. He let out a screaming meow as he fell, and landed with a hard thud.

Other than the light emanating from the hole above, the room he had fallen into was pitch black. That is, until a blinding light switched on, forcing the Kat to shield his eyes. Once adjusted, he looked around in amazement at the mechanical workshop he had fallen into.

"Ahhh," an ominous, sniveling voice spoke from the shadows. "So you've decided to drop in, yes!"

The Kat looked in the direction of the voice. His eyes lit up under his mask at the sight of his new foe. *'Who, or rather,* what *the hell is that?'*

Chapter 8

The Ninja Kat looked up in awe at the sight of the monstrous creature. Standing on an elevated platform with some sort of control panel in front of him, the villainous being resembled a spider. But he was much larger than any spider the Kat had ever seen before. He must have been at least five times the size of the Kat.

Like Slash, the arachnid was covered with a work of mechanics. His eight legs all appeared to be cut off at their squared ends, and the mechanical limbs attached on the top of the spider's back, where a similar orb of black mist protruded. Only his large, round abdomen remained untouched by the metalwork. He, too, wore a helmet on his head, though it only covered over his eyes. Two circular, beady red eyes beamed out from his helmet, while his true, fangy mandibles remained visible.

"Just who the hell are you?" The Kat demanded.

"My, how rude," the spider spoke in his creepy voice. "You barge into my domain, completely unannounced mind you, and then demand to know my name without even introducing yourself first?" The spider shook his head in disappointment. "No matter. I suppose, as your host, it should only be proper that I *do* tell you my name. My my, it's just too bad, though. I don't appear to have one."

The Kat glared at the spider, unimpressed with his mocking tone.

"You see, I am just a spider. Now, I don't know about you, but I haven't met many spiders whose mother's have ever felt the bother to actually name them. But that still doesn't solve the issue of just what it is that you should call me. So, I suppose that you may refer to me merely as the Spider."

"The Spider, huh?" The Kat asked. And then it clicked in his head. "Yeah, I've heard of you before. You're the Devil Corps' head engineer."

"Ahhh, how fascinating!" The Spider sounded amused. "To think that my name, or lack thereof, would have spread to the likes of the legendary Ninja Kat! Yes, yes, I am, indeed, the head of engineering. And, while I'm not certain exactly what it is that you expected to accomplish by infiltrating into my base of operations, I must say that I couldn't have possibly asked for more. You and your little hamster friends have provided me with such splendid opportunities to test some of my latest creations!"

"*Creations?*" The Kat asked, irritation in his voice. "Is that what you call what you did to that poor hamster?"

"Oh yes, yes! Why else do you think the Devil Corps would assign one such as me to be in charge of a military prison? Why, if not to first test out my latest inventions on our prisoners!" The Kat clenched his fists as the maniacal spider spoke his uncaring words.

"But you see," the Spider continued, "I've been watching you throughout your entire visit within my Web."

"What?" The Kat couldn't believe what he was hearing. '*But that's impossible, I was certain...*'

"Yes, yes, it's true. Oh, don't worry, your entry was indeed flawless. You did everything you were supposed to. I

40

know," the Spider chuckled, "I was watching." The Spider then lifted his front two legs. Two sharp metal spikes protruded from their squared ends. "And I watched you," he continued, typing on his control panel with his newly completed limbs, "with this!" As he hit his last key, the entire wall behind him lit up. It was a massive video screen, from which hundreds of viewpoints throughout The Web could be seen.

The Kat was dumbfounded. *'I'm certain there weren't any security cameras posted. So how can it be-?'*

"You look confused," the Spider chuckled. "And rightfully so, yes. Allow me to show you..." The Spider's words trailed off, as he turned his attention to the ground below his platform.

From the cracks in the floors and the crevices in the walls, they crawled out. Hundreds of them. Maybe even thousands. Spiders. Tiny black spiders, who together formed a wave of arachnid mass.

As they surrounded the Kat, he took a defensive position, though they stood their distance. The large screen captured the Kat's eye. He saw the thousands of different views from all of the spiders staring up at him being displayed. The sight sent a creepy chill down the Kat's spine.

"Yes, not surprising that my pets went undetected by you," the Spider spoke proudly. "As you can see, I see all that they see. And in my Web, they see *everything!*

"But as I was saying," the Spider resumed, as his army of spiders dispersed back into hiding. "When I saw who it was that decided to drop in, I couldn't have been more pleased. As I'm sure you're well aware, I have recently come into possession of quite a collection of hamsters. So naturally, when I saw a party of hamsters breaking in, I just *had* to reunite them!

"It couldn't be just *any* reunion, mind you! No, no, I had to make sure I had *just* the right hamster picked out! It just so happens that your partner looked *particularly* familiar. Yes, he looked quite similar to one of my latest test subjects. Oh, how satisfying it was to watch and find out that they were in fact *brothers!*"

The Kat was gritting his teeth. "You're a *monster*."

"Why, thank you!" the Spider retorted. "Anyways, I had another subject altogether who I decided to test on your other two friends, though sadly, that test didn't provide nearly as satisfying a result."

The Kat was shaking his head at all that he was hearing. "Why?" He asked. "Why are you even telling me all of this?"

"Why?" The Spider repeated the question. "Oh, I suppose there's no real logical reason. I just enjoy showing off my toys, especially when there's nothing you can actually do to stop me. Because, after all, whether you know it or not, you're already trapped within my Web.

"And to prove this point," the Spider said, pointing out ahead of him, "I have just one more toy that I'd like to show off to you." As a light flicked on behind the Kat, the Ninja turned around and looked on in wonder at the Spider's latest device.

It was a magnificently large tube. As the Kat peered into the half-pipe like structure, he could see no end in sight. It was as if it literally went on for forever. "*This*," the Spider proclaimed, "is the *Universal Pole!*

"I'd wager you were wondering how my creations were able to appear from out of nowhere." The Spider's words made the Kat remember the strange feeling he had when Slash was able to show up undetected. "It was with *this* that I did it. Here, allow me to demonstrate just how exactly this Universal Pole works."

The spikes retracted back into the Spider's legs, and he sprang himself from the platform. He flew through the air, landing just within the Pole. "Just watch the screen," the Spider said, "and know that no matter what, you're already too late."

'*Too late?*' the Kat thought, shooting his gaze in the direction of the large screen. '*Too late for* what?' He received his answer immediately. He couldn't believe what was being displayed on the screen. It was Flash. The barely conscious ham was being detained by a pair of canine MPs.

The Spider let out a maniacal laughter, and the Kat shot a dirty look at him. As he did, though, his rage transformed into curiosity, as the Universal Pole came to life. It's engines let out a roar, and the lights within the machine gradually rose in brilliance.

This activity only lasted for a few moments, until the light became blinding. Then, in the blink of an eye, that light was sucked back into the never ending tube. The Spider, too, had disappeared with the light.

But the Kat could still hear the Spider's laughter. It was coming from the video screen. The Kat turned to find the Spider now standing directly in front of Flash. '*What the-?!*' the Kat thought, looking up helplessly at the scene taking place on the screen. "Flash!"

"Like I said," the Spider spoke, extending the spike from his leg and pointing it towards the helpless hamster. "Too late!"

Chapter 9

No time to lose. The Kat leapt up onto the Spider's platform, sprang up to the hole in the ceiling, pulled himself up, then darted down the halls. *'Gotta make it in time!'* The Kat pushed forward. His pain was a distant memory. All that mattered was the destination. Blasting through doors. Zooming to the next. He was a bolt of lightning. Faster. Faster!

'Come on!'

He swung open the last door. He looked inside, and he froze. "No..."

The Spider had made his escape. Whatever it was he planned to do to Flash, it was too late for the Kat to stop him now. All that remained was the blood on the floor.

The Kat walked into the room and dropped to his knees. He clenched at the cloth on his trousers, staring down at Flash's blood. "Dammit." His tail twitched back and forth, and his entire body trembled as he huffed his heavy breaths. "Dammit!"

The Kat lowered his head. Staring at the floor, he watched as a tiny spider crawled past.

SMACK!

The Kat left the spider a splattered mess.

As if in response, the lights in the room shut off. They

were replaced by flashing red ones, and a deafening alarm sounded, followed shortly by the rumble of footsteps all around. Though the Kat hated to do it, it was time to go.

He slipped back into the shadows, remaining hidden as he made his escape. He managed to avoid running into any Devils on his way out, though he couldn't help but feel uneasy. After all, the Spider was obviously well aware of all of his actions.

The Ninja Kat made it back to the forest. He ran to the spot where the team had agreed to meet up. Buttons and Chippy were already there waiting for him, but strangely enough, they were not alone. Chippy was holding a tiny, lop-eared rabbit in his arms, who was happily snacking away on some cookies.

"Hey there," Buttons waved the Kat over. "We been expectin' y'all..." Butons' words trailed off as a confused look crept over his face. "Er, where's Flash?"

The Kat lowered his head, pulling his face away in shame. Buttons needn't say another word.

"Let's go," the Kat said, darting forward without another word.

Everyone remained quiet the whole way back. All except for the rabbit, who continued to chew away without a worry as he rode atop Chippy's head. Under normal circumstances, the sound would be easy enough for the Kat to ignore. But right now, it was absolutely grating.

"Would somebody shut that *thing* up!" The Kat snapped. The rabbit gulped his last bite, and then he, too, remained silent.

Buttons' eyes widened as he looked over to the rabbit, who was visibly shaken by the Kat's remarks. Chippy pulled the rabbit back into his arms and tried to console him, petting his head. When the rabbit calmed down, Buttons let out a sigh of relief.

The Kat didn't even know what to think. As he ran, he clenched his fists tighter and tighter, gritted his teeth harder and harder. His speed, too, increased significantly. He wasn't even aware that he was leaving the hamsters well behind him.

"Hey there, wait up!" Buttons yelled out. "We're not nearly as fast as you are!"

The Kat closed his eyes. He took in a deep breath and forced himself to lower his pace. It was all he could do just to keep himself under control as they ran back to base. He had nothing to say, not even to himself. His mind, his very being, was completely entrapped in rage.

So much so that, until now, he even forgot about his battle wounds. Forcing himself to calm down, his adrenaline diminished, and soon his body began to crash on him. His vision grew blurry. His legs became wobbly, until they gave out completely.

As the Kat landed hard on his chin, the hamsters skidded to a stop. "Ah man, this ain't good, Chip," Buttons said, looking down at the Kat's bloodied back. "Here, gimme that there rabbit."

Chippy handed the bunny to Buttons, then pulled the Kat up onto his back, carrying him the remainder of the way. The Kat dipped in and out of consciousness, but ultimately succumbed to rest until they made it back.

Chapter 10

Some time had passed before the Ninja Kat finally awoke. He sat up in his bed and looked down at the bandages wrapped around his body. "Tch," he huffed in annoyance. His clothes were folded neatly, sitting on a table beside his bed. They, too, had been fixed up. The Kat snatched them up and threw them on.

He got out of bed and stepped out of his room. He entered the empty meeting room and plopped down on the couch. As he stared down at the round table, he began to relive the failed mission in his head.

"Ah, you're up!" The familiar voice of the Elder Ham sprang the Kat from his troubled mindset. "We were beginning to get worried about you. You've been out of it for a while now. Ah, I know. You must be hungry! I'll have Thomasina cook something up for you."

"No," the Kat calmly declined. "I'm fine. Besides, we have some things we need to dis-"

Grr-gll...

"Um," the Kat said, looking down at his disagreeing stomach. "On second thought..."

Huck smiled, then summoned a small feast of nuts and seeds.

'I should have figured as much,' the Kat thought,

unimpressed with his unusual meal. Huck looked like he was going to laugh, but covered it up by clearing his throat.

"I'd like to be alone, if you don't mind," the Kat requested.

"Ah, yes, yes of course," Huck agreed. "I'll round up the others while you eat."

The Kat nodded his appreciation. Once the Elder left, he pulled his mask up to his mouth. He picked up one of the nuts, looking it over and sniffing it. *'Well, it's not quite chicken,'* the Kat thought, sneering, *'but it'll have to do.'*

Once the Kat finished forcing down the food, he pulled down his mask. Soon after, Huck escorted Buttons, Chippy, and their rabbit into the room. As they gathered around to sit and discuss the events that took place at The Web, the Kat found that he couldn't pull his eyes away from the lop-eared bunny.

"Ah, I suppose you must be curious about our new little friend," Huck said in response to the Kat's staring.

"Yeah," Buttons began, "we ran into this little rascal in there. He changed into this huge monster, and it looked like he was gonna try an' eat us or something. But praise the lord for Chippy here." Buttons pat his large friend on the back. "He was able to persuade this little rabbit with his cookies. Who'da thunk, right? And here I was getting' all fussy with him about it."

"Wait," the Kat said, furrowing his eyes even more curiously at the rabbit, "he *changed?*"

"Er, well, yeah..." Buttons said, looking over to the rabbit himself.

"Why don't we let our new friend tell us his tale, hmm?" Huck suggested. As all eyes turned to the rabbit, the little guy hunkered down. "It's okay, no need to be shy. We're all friends here."

48

The rabbit's wide eyes shot back and forth amongst his audience. He gulped, and he began to shake. Chippy acted quick, patting the rabbit on his head. The rabbit looked up at the large hamster's smile, which in turn helped the rabbit calm down.

"M-my... tale?" the Rabbit asked in his fragile, innocent voice.

"Yes, go on," Huck urged the rabbit.

"Well... I like running and hopping and playing, and fun! I also like carrots and hay-"

"Er," Buttons interrupted, "I don't think that's what the Elder Ham meant there, bud."

"Oh." The rabbit shriveled up into a ball. "No like talking about bad things, though."

"Ah, I know, I know," Huck said, "but it's very important that you tell us all that you can. Can you do that for us, hmm?"

"Well..." the rabbit looked over to Chippy. "For cookie?" Chippy happily pulled out a sack of cookies, and the rabbit lit up, hopping uncontrollably in his seat. "For cookie!"

The rabbit scarfed away at the chewy snacks. Meanwhile, the Kat's tail began to whip about impatiently. Huck saw this, and urged the rabbit once more to go ahead with his story.

"I was taken from Mommy and Daddy. I was put in dark place, with others who were taken from their Mommy and Daddy. There, big mean Spider man did bad things to us."

"Bad things?" the Kat asked.

"Mm-hm. He turn animals into robots. Animals no more fun after that. They become mean like Spider man."

"I see," the Kat scratched his chin.

"Spider man try and make me mean, too. But I no

turn into mean robot. I stay me."

"You stay you?" the Kat asked, puzzled. "But what about that monster Buttons said you changed into?"

"Well..." the rabbit's long ears jingled as he shuddered. "I no help, but sometimes, I change into big meany, too."

"Sometimes?"

"Mm-hm, when I get real scared. Big mean Spider man don't like, though. He make fun of me. He call me the Boogie Man."

"The Boogie Man?" The Kat asked.

"Yeah," Buttons answered for the rabbit. "We asked him his name, but he says he doesn't remember his real name. Probably a side effect from the experiments the Spider did on him. But apparently he's being called the Boogie Man. And, well, after seein' what he becomes, I've gotta say it kinda fits."

Chippy punched Buttons on the shoulder.

"Ouch! Hey, Chip, what the heck was that for?" Buttons then saw the look of horror on the rabbit's face. "Oh..."

"Mean Spider man wants make me robot, too," the rabbit continued. "But Spider man can't."

"It's probably got to do with the change," Buttons added. "Since he grows in size so much when he transforms, it's gotta be hard to come up with a robot shell that'll change in size with him."

The Kat pondered on the rabbit's tale thus far. "These experiments," he said. "What exactly are they?"

"Well, big Spider sting me with long sharp prickly thing. He push black stuff in me."

'*Black stuff?*' the Kat then thought back to the black, misty substance he found on both Slash's and the Spider's mechanical outfits. "Tell me," the Kat said, "did the Spider have a *special name* that he called this black stuff?"

"Name?" the rabbit asked.

"Yes, like he called *you* the Boogie Man. What did he call this *black stuff*?"

"Hmm," the rabbit thought. "Well, I think he called it... Magic?"

"Magic?" the Kat looked over to Huck, whose eyes widened at the mere mention. "*Black* Magic?"

"Yes!" the rabbit exclaimed. "Yes, that's it!"

The Kat shifted his body over to Huck's direction. "Before we entered The Web, I asked what it was that you were holding back from us. Flash mentioned Black Magic. I think it's time you told us everything you know about this Black Magic, Huck."

Huck brought a fist to his mouth as he cleared his throat. "Well, I guess there's no sense hiding it anymore," Huck started, shaking his lowered head in shame. "Okay then. Though I hate to do it, I'll tell you of the tragic history of Black Magic."

Chapter 11

Many generations ago, the Country of Widows was home to a variety of people. Some of these people were gifted with the ability to control the very elements that make up this land. They were able to do this using a substance known simply as Magic.

For years, these Magicians lived in harmony with the common folk, those who were unable to wield Magic. As time grew on, though, the commoners gradually grew fearful of the Magicians' great powers.

Then one day, the commoners' worst fears became a reality. A group of Magicians, in their lust for more power, stumbled upon a new kind of Magic. It was a polluted form of the elements, one which would spread corruption across the Widow Country. This Magic would go on to be known as Black Magic.

These Magicians became warped with power. They no longer saw themselves as equals with the commoners. They were clearly superior, and they felt obliged to act on their superiority. So they attempted to rule over the common folk, and any who would dare to rebel would feel the wrath of their dark power.

The common folk weren't willing to stand idly by and let the Magicians rule the lands as Gods, however. They had grown tired of being looked down upon. And so, in retaliation, these commoners banded together. And rising up from the depths of the earth, they united as one, the Corps of Devils who would take on *those would-be Gods.*

War was imminent. Though the Magicians put up a strong fight, they were surprisingly overwhelmed. They were no match for these determined Devils. It was only a matter of time before the Devils won the fight, and finally brought down those who had been corrupted by Black Magic.

But the Devils weren't yet content. They wanted to rid their country of all Magic. And so the war raged on, leading to the slaughter of thousands, most of whom were completely innocent. Men, women, even children, no one was spared in the Devils' rampage.

In the aftermath of the war, the surviving Magicians fled the country. The Devil Corps had finally rid their land of Magic. Now, it was time for them to rid the entire world of it. And so, throughout the years that followed, they continued their relentless hunt.

After many more years had passed, some began to question this seemingly endless war against Magic. With the Magicians' numbers at an alarming low, they no longer posed a threat. So the people began to wonder, was this continued slaughter of innocents really necessary?

In the end, no one was particularly proud of their achievements. What started as a crusade to rid the country of those abusing their great powers, soon became nothing more than a mindless massacre. And so, at long last, the order was made to put a stop to the war.

In their guilt, the cowards in charge passed a law that would forbid any mention of this war, of the origins of the Devil Corps, and of anything involving Magic. The hope was that the people of the Widow Country could start anew with the next generation, and forget the shameful past that lead them where they were.

The Devil Corps was revamped to work as the Widow

Country's official military force, to defend their country and protect its citizens against all threats, both foreign and domestic. That was the intent back then, at least. Oh, how times have changed.

* * *

"I was still just a young lad myself when the taboo laws were passed," Huck said, "so I had a chance to hear of those dreaded times." He shook his head. "How times have changed. I suppose there really is no more need to uphold those old laws." He lifted his head, looking to the Kat with sincerity in his eyes. "I truly do apologize for my behavior."

The Kat nodded his head.

"However," Huck continued, "this way in which our friend here says they're using Black Magic is quite unusual."

"Unusual?" the Kat asked.

"Like I said, not just *anybody* can use Magic. One must be born with the ability. And those who are can only do so by absorbing the power themselves. One cannot have Magic simply forced onto him. And yet," Huck said, looking over to the Boogie Man, "that appears to be precisely what the Devil Corps is attempting to do."

"But we've seen the stuff works on him," Buttons said. "He changed right before my eyes."

"I know, I know," Huck continued. "Buttons, do you remember the Devils who invaded our village?"

"Y-yes, sir," Buttons said.

"Those Devils were true Magicians. They were able to call upon their power all on their own. But unlike those Devils, our friend here has shown that he can't actually control this power himself."

"Maybe that's why the Spider's using machines," the Kat suggested.

"Hmm?" Huck wondered.

"If what this rabbit's saying is true, then it sounds like the Spider's more focused on fitting those prisoners in machines. After enough failed tries, he probably realized what you're saying for himself. So instead, he's using Black Magic as a way to energize his machines."

"Yeah, that makes sense," Buttons chimed in. "And since his machines turn those critters into mindless robots, he's able to completely control them."

"Hmm," Huck thought about it. "Well, I do suppose it's possible, though I haven't heard of Black Magic being used in this way before, either."

"This must be how he's networked his entire Web," the Kat added.

"What do you mean?" Huck asked.

"The Spider, he knows everything that's going on inside," the Kat explained. "There's spiders all over the place recording everything for him. And not only that, he's able to teleport anywhere inside The Web using this thing he called the Universal Pole."

"Wha..." Huck's jaw dropped. "What did you just say?"

"Teleport?" Buttons questioned. He looked over to the Boogie Man. "So *that's* how you just popped up there outta nowhere?"

"Mm-hm," the rabbit nodded.

"Well just how in the heck does something like *that* work?" Buttons wondered.

"Ah, so *that's* what they were after." Everybody turned to Huck. "This is terrible, terrible indeed."

"*What's* terrible?" the Kat asked.

"They have the *Universal Pole* at their disposal? My god," Huck's cane was trembling in his shaking hands. "It may already be too late for us to win this war."

The Kat furrowed his brows at the suggestion.

"*What?!*" Buttons nearly fell out of his seat. "You can't be serious. What d'ya mean it's too late to win the war?"

"If what I'm hearing is true," Huck started, "and this Spider has, indeed, managed to successfully build the Universal Pole, do you realize what that would mean for us?"

"No," the Kat bluntly responded. "From what I've seen, it just teleports him around The Web, how does that give the Devils any type of advantage?"

"Ah, but you're wrong," Huck responded. "The Universal Pole is much more versatile."

"What do you mean *versatile?*" the Kat asked.

"I mean, it doesn't just allow one to move from place to place within just the confines of a single building. Using that device, one could move instantly to any place he desires. Anywhere on the entire planet."

"*Anywhere?*" the Kat repeated. "So then-"

"Yes," Huck interrupted, "They'll be able to instantly appear within any village they want without warning. Your ambushes won't be a problem to them anymore."

The Kat shook his head. '*I won't be able to stop them anymore? This really is terrible. They'll have free reign to finally put their plans into motion.*' He paused, then tilted his head. "How do you know so much about this Pole?"

Huck sighed. "Ah, more secrets to reveal. Oh, the troubles of knowledge." Huck cleared his throat once more. "As you well know, we hamsters lived a more technologically advanced lifestyle than most of the other villages. Knowing this, the Devils put our people to the test while the worldwide hunt for the remaining Magicians was still in effect.

"They wanted us to build them some sort of device,

one that could instantly transport them anywhere in the world. What our people came up with was a tube, which given our village's architecture, isn't so surprising. But this wasn't just any ordinary tube. This was an everlasting tube. One that could reach to even the farthest horizons of the planet.

"Our brightest technicians worked diligently on this project. They spent years planning it out. What they ultimately came up with, though, was lauded for its controversial, some might even say hypocritical, means of use."

"What was it?" the Kat asked.

"In order for the Pole to work, one steps into the Pole, and then they just imagine where they want to be. The Pole then sucks you in, and instantly drops you off wherever it was that you imagined."

"That's it?" The Kat sounded unimpressed. "But how is that controversial?"

"Because," Huck explained, "the Pole's methods of transportation worked much in the same way that Magic works."

'*The same way Magic works?*' The Kat was intrigued.

"There were many opposed to using a 'false Magic' such as the Universal Pole in order to fight the real thing. Many felt that it would make them no better than the Magicians themselves. But still others wanted to use this Pole, in order to finally finish the hunt once and for all, by any means necessary.

"The war was called off before either side had budged, and so the actual construction of the Pole never began. The plans, however, remained locked up within our archives in Smartland."

"So even with those 'taboo laws' that passed, the

plans to the Universal Pole remained intact," the Kat concluded. "Now that I think about it, the way that you described the attack on your village was different from the ones I stopped."

"Hmm?" Huck inquired, brushing his palm through his mustache.

"The ones I stopped were on a much smaller scale. Somebody must have known that the plans to the Universal Pole still exist. That's why they used so much force, to make sure that no one, not even I, could stop them."

"Ah," Huck shook his head, "my god, you're probably right."

The group remained silent for some time. The Kat was hard at work thinking about all he had learned. With a device this powerful in their arsenal, Huck's warning that the Devils had already won certainly had merit. However, the Kat had an idea that could possibly turn the tides back in their favor.

"Huck," the Kat said, his tone sharp and precise, "I need you to tell me exactly how that thing works."

"Hmm? But I already have, haven't I?" Huck responded. "One just steps within it, and imagines where they want to go."

"It can't be that simple," the Kat argued.

"Well, I do suppose there is a bit more to it than that," Huck agreed.

'*Here we go,*' the Kat thought eagerly.

"You do have to actually *know* where it is that you want to go." The whole group stared at Huck with matching looks of confusion. "Let me try to explain. For instance, you can't just imagine yourself being at somebody's house if you don't actually know where that person lives. It doesn't work like that. You have to be able to form a very clear picture in your mind of where it is you want to be."

'Just form a clear picture, huh?' the Kat thought. *'I can do that.'*

"Well..." All eyes turned to the Boogie Man.

"Hmm? Do you have something to add, little one?" Huck asked.

"Well," the rabbit spoke, "when big Spider man put me in big machine, I didn't think of nowhere."

"Huh." Huck was stumped.

"This here Spider's supposed to be some expert engineer, right?" Buttons began. "Maybe he modified the plans to work so that he could teleport others himself. After all, how's a mindless little critter supposed to think up a place by himself, right?" Buttons looked over to the Boogie Man, holding up a peace sign with his fingers. "No offense of course, bud."

"There *was* a control panel in that room," the Kat added. "Could it be possible to activate the Pole with something like that?"

"Ah, well, I'm not too sure about that," Huck responded. "I suppose it might be possible, given how far we've come in technology since then..."

Buttons raised his index finger. "Not to mention he's probably powering it using that there Black Magic," the dwarf ham added.

"Right, right," Huck agreed, "though if he were able to work it using a control panel, he'd almost certainly have to enter in exact coordinates."

The Kat nodded his head. *'I think I've heard enough.'* He placed his paws on the round table. He pulled himself up off the couch, then looked around at his teammates.

"Hey there, what's got you all in a hurry to git on outta here?" Buttons asked.

"I'm feeling kind of tired," the Kat replied. "I think I'm gonna get a little more rest." The Kat turned his back, walking towards the door to his room.

"But wait," Buttons protested, "what about Flash?"

The Kat stopped in his tracks.

"Shouldn't we make a new plan to save him and the others?"

"Buttons," Huck tried to hush the younger hamster.

"But Elder-"

"No," the Elder Ham spoke firmly. "That's enough."

The Kat took in a deep breath. Without saying another word, he continued to his room.

"Hmm," Huck laid his chin against the top of his cane. He squinted his eyes, as if trying to read the Kat's thoughts.

The Kat closed the door behind him. He stood silently within his room, the only sound coming from the bees buzzing up above. *'Tonight's the night,'* he thought, punching his fist into his palm. *'I'm going to end this war* tonight!'

Chapter 12

That night, after all of the hamsters had fallen asleep, the Ninja Kat snuck out of the tree base by himself. He made his way through the forest, all the way back to The Web, where he knelt down just within the treeline bordering the prison grounds and played out his plan within his mind. Content, he took in a deep breath and reached back for his sword.

He sprang to his feet. Racing forward, he sliced ahead, cutting an opening through the fence. He rushed through the plains without a care about staying hidden. He flew through the air, barging through the door with a hard kick.

Standing at the doorway, the Kat stared face to face with a squadron of Devils inside. '*Okay,*' he thought, a calm confidence in his voice. '*Lets do this.*'

The canine in the lead pointed out at the Kat and snarled. "Get him!" The first line of Devils charged forward, but the Kat made quick work of them with precise strikes.

He advanced to the next line, who split up and surrounded the Kat, forcing him to fight off the Devils from all sides. He kept up for as long as he could, but the enemy's numbers were just too much. So the Kat reached back, grabbing a pair of smoke grenades. He dropped them, and the smoke spread quickly, covering the hallway within a black cloud.

The Kat dropped down, crawling across the floor through his opponents' legs. As he passed by, he heard the enemies' blades clashing with the ground behind him, just missing their target. When the Kat broke out of the smoke, he rolled to the next hall, slamming the hatch shut and locking it behind him.

Then he turned around to find another roomful of Devils waiting for him.

'*Tch. Here we go again.*'

The Kat reached back, grabbing two handfuls of throwing stars, then sprang into the air. Staring down at the legion of Devils, he threw his stars about, taking out as many as he could.

Landing within the circle of his fallen foes, the Kat darted forward, sword in hand. He slashed his way through the pack, until a bulldog up ahead shot a black bolt from his hand. The Kat retaliated, striking the bolt with his sword. But as the Kat charged towards the bulldog, the darkness spread over his blade. The Kat attacked with an upward slash, but the top half of his sword disintegrated upon contact.

The Kat's eyes widened. '*What the...*'

The bulldog smiled, powering up an orb of Black Magic in his hand. The bulldog punched the Kat in the gut, then as the Kat fell down to his back, a pair of Devils pounced on top of him. They pulled the Kat up, holding him in the air by his arms. Smirking, the bulldog powered up his hand, rearing for another blow. But the Kat lifted his legs, wrapping them around the bulldog's neck. The Kat then twirled aside, dragging his captors down with him.

Freeing himself, the Kat took a moment to survey the scene. '*I'm not gonna be able to keep this up for much longer,*' he thought, clutching his stomach.

The remaining Devils halted their approach. They each held out their palms, pointing them down at the Kat. He watched only long enough to see their hands begin to glow a black aura.

'Okay, time to go.' The Kat high tailed it to the next hatch, just making it to the door and slamming it shut as the blasts of Black Magic barreled against the wall.

As the Kat rushed forward, he found the following halls to be as empty as he remembered from his first visit. *'That actually went a lot easier than I anticipated,'* the Kat thought suspiciously. *'Even with their Magic, those Devils barely put up a fight.'*

The Kat made sure to pay closer attention as he approached the hole in the floor this time, sliding to a halt just at the hole's edge. He peered inside, but all was dark within. He hopped in, grabbing hold of the edge, then swung from the ceiling, landing gracefully onto the elevated platform.

As he looked down at the Spider's control panel, he tilted his head. *'Now to just figure out which button turns the thing on.'* A lever on the side of the controls caught his eye. He scratched his chin as he looked it over. It was pointed upwards, where it read the word 'INCREASE'. The lower end of the lever read 'DECREASE'.

'Increase and decrease?' The Kat thought quizzically. Before he could figure the controls out, though, the blinding lights flicked on throughout the workshop.

"Ahh, so you came back after all." The Spider was standing just outside the Universal Pole. He had two feline Devils in front of him, armed with swords and ready for combat. "Though it's certainly a coincidence that you decided to drop in right now. I was actually just on my way to pay you a visit, yes."

'What? He can't mean-'

The Spider faced the Pole's entrance. "Still, I wouldn't want your hamster friends to feel left out. So I suppose I'll just pick them up and bring them back to my Web." The Spider let out a maniacal laugh as the Universal Pole came to life. The Kat looked around furiously, and the two Devils made their move.

'Damn. Think fast.' The Kat's eyes were drawn back to the lever. *'I won't be able to stop him in time, but maybe...'* As he grabbed hold of the lever, the cats sprang up. They landed on the railing, looking down at the Kat.

The two felines lifted their swords face down.

The Pole's light consumed the Spider.

The felines struck down.

The Ninja Kat pulled the 'DECREASE' lever.

Then the blades stabbed into the control panel, rendering it useless.

When the light sucked the Spider into the Pole, the Kat saw that it moved noticeably slower than before. *'It's as I thought. By slowing the Pole down, I've bought myself some time. But still,'* the Kat turned his attention to the two feline Devils, who had pulled their swords back out of the destroyed controls. *'I've got to hurry.'*

The felines pounced at him. The Kat kicked the first feline in midair, sending him sailing over the railing. Then he lifted his broken sword, defending against the second's attack. As the Devil applied pressure, the Kat's sword began to waver. But the Kat powered back and managed to force the enemy to drop his sword.

The Kat picked it up, then pointed his two weapons at the enemy feline. The Devil snarled, revealing his sharp claws. He then swiped out, but the Kat sidestepped, smacking his hilt against the Devil's head and knocking the feline out.

The Kat sheathed his broken sword, then hopped off the platform, where the first feline staggered back to his feet. He chopped the Devil on the neck, putting him out cold before taking his sword as well.

Now wielding two new weapons, the Kat stepped up to the Pole himself. *'Now to just imagine where I want to be.'* The Kat closed his eyes, concentrating. *'With the Spider on his way to the hamsters' hideout, that puts my original plan in a damper. So then, I guess the hideout? Unless...'*

The Kat opened his eyes, staring deep into the endless pipe. *'It's kind of a long shot, but if this works, it'll definitely be worth it.'* The Kat pictured a place in his mind. He made his desired destination as clear as he possibly could, and then the blinding light shined. The light latched on to him, and before he knew it, he was being sucked into the Pole.

'Here we go.'

Chapter 13

The Ninja Kat felt as if he had dived into a pool of water. He was being flushed through the pipework, unable to resist. As he traveled deeper, the light began to disperse, flowing ahead in waves against the walls of the Universal Pole.

No longer blinded, the Kat made an effort to see what lay ahead in his path. At first, all he could see were rings of light. As his eyes adjusted, though, he was able to make out a certain eight-legged figure up ahead. *'Perfect.'*

The Kat made an attempt to run. As he lifted his feet, though, his body wobbled uncontrollably. He was moving at too fast a speed to run against the sides of the Pole. *'Damn, what do I do?'* The Kat slipped. He stumbled forward, but caught his balance as he pressed his fist to the ground.

The Kat stared at the figure up ahead. With determined eyes, he propelled himself forward. Gliding down the Pole, he alternated his feet, keeping them pressed against the ground as he seamlessly skated forward. With the tube's natural pull boosting his speed, it wasn't long before he managed to catch up with the Spider.

"Ahh, a clever trick that was, slowing down the Pole like you did," the Spider quipped, as the Kat skated up alongside him. "And yet, unless you're able to stop me now, it was all for naught."

The Kat readied his swords. "That's kind of the idea."

The Spider swiped one of his metal legs at the Kat, but The Kat blocked it, just as the Spider extended its spike. The Spider slid ahead, twisting around to face the Kat head on. He stood on his four rear legs, shooting the spikes out from his remaining limbs. He attacked with a barrage of slashes and stabs. It took everything the Kat had to block them all, a feat that would have been impossible using only one sword.

"I *am* curious," the Spider began, "why was it that you came straight to the Universal Pole? Shouldn't you be attempting another hopeless rescue mission?" The Spider retracted the spikes. He turned his back, gliding further ahead down the Pole. "You can't really be planning *that*."

'What is he going on about now?' the Kat wondered.

"Surely," the Spider continued, "even with the element of surprise that the Pole offers, you don't really believe you actually stand a chance against *him*, do you?"

'What?!' The Kat couldn't believe what he was hearing. *'Was my plan really that obvious?'* As the Spider let out a maniacal laughter, the Kat shook his head. *'Can't worry about that now. I've gotta stop this Spider before it's too late.'*

The Kat pushed forward, catching up with his foe. He slashed out at the Spider's legs, but a show of sparks spewed as the metal clashed, forcing the Kat to distance himself.

'Tch, this isn't gonna work,' the Kat thought, noticing no visible damage done to the Spider. *'I've got to land a hit on his real body if I'm gonna stop him.'*

The Kat turned his head upwards. *'I wonder...'* He skated to the side, riding up the wall of the Pole. He continued up until he stood on the Pole's ceiling, his feet never peeling away even standing upside down. The Kat looked down at the Spider, now riding along parallel to him.

"Ahh, what a clever kitty you are indeed, yes," the Spider commented, lifting his eyes up to the Kat.

The Kat aimed for the Spider's large abdomen. He sprang down, but the Spider lifted his rear legs. A burst of black flames shot out, driving the Spider forward and causing the Kat's blades to stab the Pole, just missing their mark.

The Kat was only able to pull up his swords before the Pole's force took its toll. He tumbled around like a rag doll, trying desperately to recapture his bearings.

The Spider jumped the gun on the Kat, shooting a string of webbing at him. It wrapped around the Kat's swords, tying them together. The Spider then pulled the Kat towards him, stabbing out with his spike. But the Kat tugged on his swords, cutting them free, and he blocked the stab just in time.

Then, looking down at the Spider's metal limb, an idea struck the Kat. 'That's it!'

As the Spider stabbed out again, the Kat dropped one of his swords. He dodged the attack, latching onto the Spider's leg with his free hand. He pulled himself onto the leg, crawling across the fidgeting arachnid's metalwork, making his way towards the head. There, he lifted his sword, ready to stab down at the revealed portion of the Spider's face.

"Well it certainly looks like you've got me beat, yes," the Spider sounded amused. "I don't suppose it's any use asking you to spare me, if only for a moment?"

"And why would I do that?" the Kat demanded, "So you can turn even more innocent hamsters into mindless machines?"

"Oh, that." the Spider shook his head. "No, no, we're not actually heading towards the hamster's hideout. My, I'm not even sure where it is."

The Kat was stunned. "What are you talking about?" He pressed his sword against the Spider's flesh. "Explain yourself."

"I only told you that so you'd follow me, of course."

The Kat grunted in annoyance. "Then if not the hamster's hideout, where?"

"Ahh, well it's a surprise you see," the Spider responded. "That's why I ask that you spare me. I just *have* to see the look on your face when we get there. Though, I suppose that'll be a challenge all its own, what with that mask hiding your face and all."

'*A surprise?*' the Kat thought. '*Tch, I've had it with this guy.*' The Kat lifted his sword, ready to stab down. As he did, though, the waves of light on the Pole's walls were converging up ahead. Curiosity caught the better of the Kat, who marveled at the Pole's activity. The two rode straight into the blinding brilliance, closing in on their destination.

"It's as I told you before," the Spider laughed. "You're already trapped within my Web."

Chapter 14

In the blink of an eye, the two were released from the Universal Pole's grasp. They were dropped off within a corridor of The Web. As the Spider's feet made their sudden re-acquaintance with immobile ground, the Kat was tossed from the arachnid's body. He twirled in midair, landing with a kneel.

Facing down, he saw a pair of familiar long, razor sharp claws dangling to the floor on either side of him. Holding his breath, the Kat lifted his head. He was staring face to face Slash. *'But... how?'*

"Ahh, yes, you certainly do seem surprised thus far," the Spider said. "The last time you saw this one, he *did* appear to be quite dead, yes. And he very well would have been, had I not instructed him to end things when I did."

As the Spider spoke, the Kat noticed a rather large crack on the top of Slash's helmet. From it, some of his light brown fur was sticking out.

"Your little friend was doing a number with that saw of his. It appeared to me that he was actually trying to free this one from his robotic shell." The Spider shook his head. "Tsk tsk, we couldn't have that, though. So I had this one put an end to your friend's feeble rescue attempt with a quick stab to the chest. But, of course, you already know all about that.

"However, the damage had already been done," the Spider continued. "So I decided to shut this one down before I had a chance to reanalyze him for myself."

Slash lifted an arm. He pointed his claws in the Kat's direction, or so it seemed. The Kat noticed the mecha-ham was actually pointing over the Kat's head, towards something else behind him. "Ahh, would you look at that. It would appear that this one wants to show you something, yes."

Gripping his sword tightly, the Kat cautiously turned around. All that stood behind him, though, was the Spider, in all his mechanical glory. "You see, you left before you had a chance to discover the fate of your little hamster friend."

"What are you talking about, his fate?" The Kat gritted his teeth. "I saw *exactly* what you did to Flash."

"Ahh, but did you really?" The Spider shot a web up to the ceiling. He crawled up the webbing, looking down at the Kat gleefully. As the Kat watched on, he realized that, standing behind the Spider, there was another new character.

This newcomer was another mechanized hamster. His design differed from Slash's, though. He had the same robotic arms, but he lacked the extensively long claws. And his helmet covered only his nose and mouth, leaving the top of his head completely out in the open.

The Kat's eyes were drawn to the hamster's.

His sword slipped through his fingers, falling to the ground. Just as his jaw had fallen. Just as his heart had sunk.

The hamster's eyes were filled with pain.

"... Flash?"

"Yes, yes, there it is!" The Spider laughed. "*That*'s the look I was waiting for!"

"You..." the Kat clenched his fists. "You *monster*."

"Yes, we've already established that," the Spider

retorted. "Ahh, but you should be proud of your friend here. He's got a much stronger will than any of my previous creations. You see, despite all of my efforts, I just couldn't manage to extract the whereabouts of the hamster's hideout from him. In fact, as we speak, he's *still* desperately holding that information away from me.

"However," he continued, "since he's focusing so strongly on holding that information back, that leaves the rest of his being free for me to control as I please. My, what an interesting subject he's turned out to be."

'*Flash*,' the Kat was shaken by the Spider's words.

"And now, to put my new creation to work." The Spider turned to Flash. "As your first order of business," he said, pointing down to the Kat, "reveal his true face. Let us see what he has to hide under that mask of his."

Flash lifted an arm. He fired out three small, bullet-like claws. They scraped the side of the Kat's mask, leaving tear marks in their wake.

The Kat dipped for his sword, but as he did, Slash's shadow loomed over behind him. So he kicked back, knocking Slash backwards.

Flash rushed towards the Kat, kicking his sword out of the way and driving his knee into the Kat's chin. The Kat fell back, landing on Slash's feet. Slash pulled the Kat up, pressing his claws to the Kat's neck.

Trapped, all the Kat could do was helplessly pull his head away as Flash reached down. But the hamster grabbed hold, tugging the black mask off.

"My my, who would have ever thought *you* were the Ninja Kat?" The Spider sounded genuinely surprised, staring down at the scowling face of the brown tabby cat. "Okay boys, playtime's over. Lock *her* away."

Chapter 15

In breaking news, the terrorist known as 'The Ninja Kat' has been captured. She was caught in the act at a military prison, which remains unnamed. Reportedly, the military prison was her next targeted attack.

"I'm just glad we managed to stop her before it was too late," spoke Colonel Bullet, who looks over the military prison. "I shudder to think of the damage that could have been caused had she succeeded with this latest attack."

The terrorist was revealed to be a former member of the Devil Corps. She went AWOL not long before her attacks began several months ago. She had been attacking squads of Devils, dispatched throughout the Widow Country on various training exercises.

"It is disturbing that the terrorist turned out to be one of our own," Bullet added. "I just can't imagine what could have driven her to the point that she'd attack her own people." When asked about the possibility of the terrorist being a foreign spy, the Colonel didn't rule out the idea, but refrained from making further comments.

The terrorist, who originally resided in Highland, has yet to make an official statement. Her name is...

Charlie tossed his newspaper aside. "That's a load of bull."

He took a sip of his drink, sitting alone in a dimly lit bar. He was growling under his breath, his crooked tail whipping wildly.

"Hey Charlie!" Rocky sprang up beside his mentor. "Did ya see it, Charlie? Huh, Charlie? Can you believe it, Charlie? I can't! Who would'a thought, Charlie? That she's-"

Charlie wrapped his paw around the gray cat's neck. "Not another word from you, got it?" Rocky gulped in response. Charlie let go, returning to his drink.

"R-right, Charlie. Sorry about that, not another word out of me. Nope. Uh-uh. Nada. Zippo. No siree-"

Charlie snapped a killing gaze at the young cat. He immediately shut his mouth, sulking down silently into the chair next to Charlie.

The black tabby shook his head, downing his drink. He asked for another one, just as he was joined by Stan.

"So, I'm guessing you heard then, huh?" The black and white cat asked in his high pitched tone.

Charlie snorted into his drink.

"H-hey Rocky," Stan said, "I think he needs some time alone."

"Oh, uh," Rocky began, but zipped his mouth shut before he would regret it. He nodded his head repeatedly instead, following his larger friend to another table.

Charlie slammed his mug on the counter. He gripped it so tight that the glass began to crack. "Dammit."

He picked up the newspaper. He stared at the picture of the unmasked Ninja Kat, of the young, brown tabby who glared with her piercing green eyes. "Velcro..."

He crumpled the paper in his hands. "You idiot."

'*How could I let this happen?*'

The Kat sat silently, playing out the events in her head.

'*From the moment I stepped foot in this prison, the Spider saw through all of my moves. Could he have really planned all of this from the start?*'

The Kat reminisced on her conversation with the Spider: "*Why are you even telling me all of this?*"

"*Oh, I suppose there's no real logical reason. After all, you're already trapped within my Web.*"

'*Now I know why he told me so much. He saw that I was working with the hamsters. He let me leave the Web so that I'd learn about the Universal Pole. And using the Pole as his bait, he lured me back. And I just walked right into his trap.*

'*But, then again, why did he even let me leave at all? He had me right there, wouldn't it have made more sense to just lock me up from the get go? Did he really go through all that trouble just to embarrass me?*

'*No, that just doesn't make sense. The Spider's proven he's much too smart to mess around and put his plans at risk. There was a reason he let me escape. There had to be. But what was it... !*'

The Kat's eyes lit up.

'*That rabbit. He seemed innocent enough, but do we really know? Maybe it's an act, and he's actually working alongside the Spider. He knows of the hamsters' location now, after all.*

'*Then again, he did seem pretty sincere to me. But if he's not a spy, then...*'

The Kat thought back to what Buttons had said before. "*He changed into this huge monster, and it looked like he was gonna try an' eat us or something.*"

'*Is that what the Spider's planning? Not to learn of their* location, but to wipe it out using that rabbit? After all, the rabbit admitted he couldn't control it. And who's to say Chippy won't run out of treats at the wrong time?'

The Kat let out a sigh.

'I underestimated that Spider. I completely fell for his trap. Maybe he's even right about that, too.'

"You don't really believe you actually stand a chance against him, do you?" As the Spider's words rang in the Kat's head, the image of that particular canine's vicious eyes gleamed in her mind.

'Tch, none of that really matters while I'm cooped up in this cell, though. I've gotta figure a way out of here first. Then I can worry about what's going on outside.'

"You're awful quiet over there," an elderly voice broke the silence.

With the twitch of an ear, the Kat was snapped back into reality. She sat in the corner of her cramped cell. Her arms were wrapped around her legs, her head held low. While she continued to stare out into space, her grim surroundings suddenly became visible to her once more.

"I know what you're thinking, child." the elderly woman in the neighboring cell continued. "Long as I been here, lord knows I've thought it myself. But believe me. When the Spider says you're trapped here, he means it."

The Kat huffed. She tried to ignore the old woman and return to her thoughts, but the elder wasn't through with her yet.

"Of course, there's something different about you, isn't there?" the elder continued. "You may not hear it, but people here been talkin' about you. Even within these walls, your name is spoken highly of. Or, at least the name you go by under that mask.

"You do have a real name, don't ya, child?" She

paused, waiting for a response.

The Ninja Kat offered nothing.

"Heh, okay. Keep giving me the silent treatment, but I'm still gonna keep on talkin' anyhow. Right now, the word of your capture is likely being spread all over. Course, you know the Devil Corps' gonna add their own spin to it."

The Kat's eyebrow flickered. The thought of her capture being known intrigued her. She toyed with the idea of someone on the outside possibly breaking her out.

'Would the hamsters really attempt such a dangerous mission without me?' She quickly shook that thought out of her head. *'No, I'd hate for them to take such a risk just to save me. I've been enough of a burden to them as it is. There's got to be another way.'*

"Anyways," the elder continued, "I have something I'd like to share with you. But first I'd like to properly introduce myself. I'm Maggie, and like you, I, too, was once a member of the Devil Corps."

The Kat shifted her eyes towards Maggie's voice.

"Now, even if you don't have nothin' to say to me, I feel I should share my story with you. Because you see, child, I was fighting this war long before you were even breathing."

Chapter 16

"I guess it all starts in the beginning," Maggie began. "I had a normal enough puppy-hood. Decent upbringing, with a good, lovin' family, always there to support me. But none more so than my little sis, Molly.

"You'd never guess we were sisters just by looking at us. See, I come from a dalmatian family. Nothin' special about that, except that Molly didn't look like any ordinary dalmatian. She was black as night all over, not a spot on her. She looked like a different breed of dog, that's for sure, but I loved her all the same.

"Growing up as a young pup, me and my little sis were inseparable. We were the best of friends, and we always did everything together. And that included joining the Devil Corps. Our family wasn't too keen on the idea of us signing up. My sis, though, she stayed by my side all the way. But in a strange twist of irony, the military ended up being what finally tore us apart.

"You see, growing up, I was always a bit more gifted than Molly in certain respects. Just a little bit smarter. Just a little bit stronger, which was kind of funny, since she was always so much bigger than me. But I was clearly ahead of her, just enough that I ended up leaving her behind.

"While I was being promoted and placed in charge of

my own units, Molly was left struggling at the bottom, still doing grunt work. I could tell she wasn't happy about it, but I never would have imagined she'd go to the lengths she did to change all that.

"Molly turned to alternate sources of power. *Illegal* sources. And using this new power of hers, she was able to falsely convince her superiors to move her up the ranks as well. But I just knew something was off. She just wasn't herself anymore. It wasn't just that she was unhappy like before. Now, she seemed bitter. Like she had some sort of a score to settle.

"I confronted her about it, but she just accused me of being jealous of her new found glory. Now, suddenly, I wasn't the only success story of the family, and I was just going to have to deal with that.

"Her arrogance worried me, and so, though I felt bad to do it, I decided to snoop on my little sis. And that's when I learned the worst. The source of her false power. She had been using Black Magic this whole time.

"I called her out on it. I demanded that she confess to her crimes, or else I'd turn her in myself. But she wouldn't listen. And she couldn't have me ruin this for her. So she threatened to shut my mouth, *permanently* if need be.

"And so we fought." Maggie paused, as if trying to recapture her breath. "And while the Black Magic certainly made her stronger, even so, I still outmatched her, if only barely. But no matter what I did, she just wouldn't stop. She just wouldn't stay down. And so she left me no choice."

The Ninja Kat could hear as Maggie tried her hardest to fight back the tears. "It's the last thing I would have ever wanted. But it became do or die for both of us at that point. And, like always was the case with me and her, I came out on top.

"I was imprisoned for my crime, stripped of my title of Devil. And I've been here ever since. Lord knows that not a day goes by where I don't wish that I could go back to that moment and make things right."

There was a long pause after Maggie had finished talking. Drawn in by the dog's story, the Ninja Kat finally felt compelled to fill that void of silence.

"You said that your sister was using Black Magic. How did she come across it?"

"Oh, so you're willing to talk after all." Maggie sniffed. "And it's funny you should ask that question, seein' as you probably already know the answer. Molly was taught the ways of Black Magic by someone else who's used it to rise through the ranks.

"He's used it to rise all the way to the very top, in fact, corrupting all of those below him in his ascent. And now he's the one calling all the shots these days. He's the one who initiated this secret war. He started way back then with my little sis, and has since moved on to destroying entire villages.

"I'm sure that you know who I'm talking about by now, right child?"

As she spoke those words, the large, musclebound canine's image appeared clearer than ever within the mind of the Ninja Kat. *"The Devil Dog."*

"That's right."

The two sat in silence for some time after that. The Kat could hear Maggie quietly crying in the next cell, no longer holding her tears back. Telling that story clearly wasn't easy for her, but after hearing it, the Kat understood why she felt the need to do so.

The Kat inhaled a deep breath. Letting it out slowly, she closed her eyes.

"You asked me before what my name was."

Maggie sniffed her tears away. "Hmm, you say something, child?"

"Yeah," the Kat said. She opened her eyes, and prepared to open her heart. "My name is Velcro."

Chapter 17

Once upon a time, Velcro used to be a very playful little kitten. She'd always go off on her own, fighting off imaginary villains and pretending she was a great warrior. She had big dreams back then. Some day, she really *was* going to be a great warrior. And today was the day that she'd take her first step towards that dream.

On this day, she set her imagination aside, opting for the real thing. She didn't want to start off too big, though. So, crawling through the tall grass, making sure her presence remained undetected, she stalked out her first victim.

It was a lizard. A small, green lizard, who itself blended in fairly well with the environment. Velcro slowly approached. As she moved, the grass shifted. The lizard stopped in it's tracks, looking around for any threats. Noticing nothing out of the ordinary, it continued to scurry about.

Velcro crept forward, her eyes never leaving their target. When it appeared that the lizard had let its guard down, Velcro scrunched down, ready to pounce at her victim.

"Rrrrrrowr!"

Velcro turned towards the sound of the growl, but it was too late. A black tabby pounced out through the grass, tackling her down. Pinning Velcro to the ground, the black cat grinned in amusement, his youthful blue eyes glowing.

Velcro's eyes had shot wide open. She was breathing heavily, still frightened from the sudden attack. Upon realizing who her attacker was, she shook the fear from her face, scowling at her perpetrator.

"*Charlie!*" she hissed.

"Got ya again, sis," Charlie laughed. "You're gonna have to do better than that."

Velcro shoved her brother off of her, huffing through her nose as she sat up. "*Grr*, I'm telling Daddy when he gets home."

"*What?* Gah, you tattle tail," Charlie whined. "You know they don't let tattle tails join the Devil Corps, right?"

"You shut up," Velcro snapped. "I *am* gonna be a Devil someday. Just like Daddy. And not only that, but I'm gonna be the best Devil ever."

"Who, you?" Charlie snickered. "Yeah right, you idiot. You can't even catch a little lizard." The two looked over to the lizard, watching as it frantically scurried away. "And besides, you're way too easy to sneak up on. You'd be taken out in seconds in a real fight. Ha, so much for being the best Devil ever."

Velcro was growing frustrated with her brother. She dug her claws into the ground, whipping her tail wildly. "*Grr*, just leave me alone, Charlie. *You're* the idiot."

"*What?*" Charlie began to retort back, until he heard his name being called out in the distance. "Heh, whatever. You're no fun anyways," he said, heading towards his group of friends waving him over. "Just keep playing with yourself, Velcro. You're much better at catching things that aren't real."

Velcro watched as Charlie ran off to play with his friends. A gust of wind blew by, brushing the grass into her view. When the tall blades settled, Charlie and his friends were long out of sight.

Velcro's jaw began to tremble, but only for a moment. She sucked it in, pounding her fist against the ground. *'I'll show you, Charlie. I* will *be the best Devil ever.'*

She rolled back onto her stomach, sneaking through the grass until she found the green lizard once more. She reared her legs back, waiting for the moment to strike. Then she sprang forward, landing with her claws outstretched. When she lifted her paws, though, all that lay below them was dirt.

She looked up and watched as the lizard scrambled away scott free. Frowning, she dropped her head, letting the grass blow in her face.

Later that day, Velcro wandered home. It was a cozy little wooden house, and was surrounded by a meadow of grass. She sat at the table, where she pulled out a pencil and her drawing book. Sitting with her hand resting on her cheek, she scribbled away. She would often draw her imaginary villains, what they really looked like. She'd capture her battles with them on paper, and she always stood victorious over them in the end.

Today, though, she couldn't muster her hand to draw that last victory pose. Today, when she tried to think of how she'd defeated her latest opponent, nothing came to mind. She pressed her pencil to the paper, but she didn't have the will to move it. So, she let the pencil slip from her grip, falling to the table and rolling off onto the floor.

Velcro shoved her drawing book away. She placed her arms on the table, lying her head down on them. Then her ear twitched at the sound of jingling keys unlocking the front door. She popped her head up, smiling, and ran excitedly to the door.

"Daddy!" Just as the door swung open, she leaped into the arms of her father.

"Whoa, hey precious," her father said, pulling his face away as she tried to lick him. "What's got you all worked up?"

"Please teach me how to fight, Daddy. Please!"

"Huh, what's this all of a sudden?"

"I wanna be a Devil, Daddy. Just like you. But Charlie said I can't do it, since I don't know how to fight. So please, Daddy, teach me. Please?"

"Well, I don't know," her father said, putting Velcro back on the ground. "You're still pretty young."

Velcro looked up at her father with big bulging, pleading eyes. Her paws were clasped together, held up in a begging manner.

Her father let out a sigh. "Oh alright. I guess it wouldn't hurt to show you a few things."

Velcro gasped, wrapping her arms around her father with a beaming smile on her face. "Oh thank you, Daddy. Thank you thank you thank you!"

"Hey now, easy," her father said. "If I'm going to do this for you, you're going to have to promise to be nice to your brother for me."

"*What?*" Velcro pulled herself away from her father. "But he's the one who's always mean to *me*."

"Nope, we've been over this," her father said sternly, placing his hands on her shoulders. "It works both ways. I'll talk to him about being nicer to you, too. But I want you to promise me you'll do your part."

Velcro looked away, pursing her mouth. "Fine."

"Good," her father said, rustling the fur on her head. "Now if you really want me to teach you, just know this. I'm not going to hold your hand if you want to learn how to fight for real. So, tomorrow morning, you're going to have to wake yourself up, bright and early, and I'll be waiting for you at the Twin Trees. Got it?"

"Got it!" Velcro smiled big, showing off her fangs with glee.

Chapter 18

The next morning, Velcro sat patiently on the bench at the Twin Trees. It was a large, grassy area off in the outskirts of Highland. It was named as such due to the two enormous trees that stood on either end of the long plain, their shadows combined blocking out all of the sun up above.

In the hot summer days, it was a nice cool place that Velcro's father liked to come out to, to get some personal training done. On this morning, as her father walked onto the training field, he looked shocked to find that his daughter had actually beaten him there.

"Wow, you're here already, huh? You must really be serious about this."

Velcro only smiled her response.

"Heh, alright," he said. "Well, lets get started then."

Velcro hopped off the bench, ready to start her first day of training.

Without warning, her father threw a punch right at her face. Instinctively, Velcro raised her arms up, cowering from the attack, squeezing her eyes tight.

She remained frozen in that silly pose as she awaited the inevitable strike. But it never came. When Velcro opened her eyes, she saw that her father's fist had stopped less than an inch away from her face.

"Lets start out with the basics," her father said, with a smirk and a wink.

The two worked together through the rest of the morning. With someone there to guide her, Velcro found it easier to pick up than she'd originally thought. Her father appeared equally as impressed by his daughter's progress.

"You're kind of a natural at this," her father commented.

"You really think so?" Velcro smiled.

As they continued their training, Charlie and his friends found their way onto the field. They were tossing a ball around, and didn't appear to notice Velcro or her father. Velcro stopped, watching the boys having a good time.

Charlie then noticed the two for the first time. He paused his game, staring at them curiously. Velcro pulled her head away, crossing her arms with a huff.

"Hey now," her father said, "what did we discuss yesterday?"

Velcro opened an eye, peeking over at Charlie and his friends.

"Why don't you go over and play with them?" her father suggested.

"What?" Velcro couldn't believe her father's words. "No way. I want to keep training."

"Well, I think we're done for the day," her father responded, "so you can play with your brother now, and we'll continue tomorrow."

"Awww," Velcro whined.

"Hey, remember our deal, Velcro," her father spoke firmly.

"Oh fine." Velcro kicked up at the grass, as her father walked away shaking his head.

Holding her head low, Velcro walked up towards the

group of boys. They put their game on hold as she got closer. Charlie placed his fists on his hips, tilting his head. "What do *you* want?"

"I..." Velcro started, looking to the ground. She lifted her eyes, staring into her brother's. Then she scowled at him. "Nothing."

"Heh," Charlie laughed. "Whatever."

Velcro twirled away, storming off with her fists clenched tight as the boys resumed their game. *'I'm sorry, Daddy,'* she thought, staring down at the grass with disappointed eyes. *'I promise I'll try harder next time.'*

Velcro continued her hand-to-hand training with her father throughout the months that followed. It wasn't long before he began showing her more advanced techniques. Velcro truly was a natural talent.

"Now today," her father said, "I'm going to teach you the most important lesson you'll learn in combat training."

'Oh man, I can't wait,' Velcro thought, shaking with excitement. *'I wonder what it could be?'*

"And that lesson is this," her father continued, holding an index finger in the air. *"Never* use any of these techniques that I've taught you."

'What?!' Velcro's jaw had dropped. "B-but-"

"Let me explain," her father interrupted. "I don't want you going around picking fights, you got that? Everything I've taught you is to be used only if absolutely necessary. If you can avoid fighting, do so. Got it?"

"Yeah," she said, rolling her eyes in annoyance. "Got it."

"I'm serious," he continued, "I don't want you getting hurt."

"But if I use what you've taught me, I *won't* get hurt,

Daddy."

"Nope, don't do that," he warned. "I want you to stay out of trouble. I've already got my hands full enough with your brother."

Velcro let out a huff. "Fine," she conceded.

"Good. Now that we've got that out of the way," her father reached behind him. Velcro's eyes lit up as he unsheathed his sword, holding it out in front of him. "Today, lets start a *new* kind of training."

He turned the blade towards himself, holding the hilt out to his daughter. She grabbed the sword from her father, staring wondrously at the shiny blade, swinging it out in front of her.

Her father then pulled out a second sword. He swung it at Velcro's, sending it flying out of her hands. *"Hey."*

"What, are you done already?" he teased.

"No." Velcro picked her sword up off the ground. Gripping the hilt tightly, she took a weak fighting stance.

Her father smirked, repositioning her body to a more proper stance. "There we are," he said, admiring his tenacious little girl. *"Now* you're ready to fight."

Chapter 19

Some nights later, Velcro, Charlie, and their father sat down for dinner. Their father had arranged a feast of chicken and various fish. The two siblings were delighted by the sight at first. But as they took their seats, they realized what this meant, and both cats couldn't keep from frowning.

"You're goin' away again, aren't you?" Charlie asked.

"It's that obvious, huh?" Their father sighed as he took his own seat.

"We always have a big meal like this just before you go away," Charlie said.

"Yeah, I guess we do, don't we?" He shook his head. "Sorry about this, kids. I know you two hate it when I leave, but believe me, you don't hate it nearly as much as I do."

"Whatever," Charlie said, pushing his plate away. "I'm not even hungry anyways." He stood up out of his chair and headed towards the door.

"*Charlie,*" Velcro chided.

"Hey, just where do you think you're going?" His father demanded.

"I'm not the one who's going anywhere," Charlie responded, walking out the door. "*You* are." He slammed the door behind him.

Velcro and her father sat in silence. For several

minutes, neither had touched their food. "Eat up, precious," her father urged.

Hesitating, Velcro took a bite out of her chicken. Once the delicious, juicy meat hit her tongue, she couldn't hold back anymore. She gorged down her food, though her father continued to ignore his own.

"I really worry about him sometimes," her father started. "Velcro, when I'm gone, I want you to look out for him, okay?"

Velcro stopped eating in mid-bite, staring strangely at her father.

"I know it's hard for you, and I know you two don't really get along. But I need you to be the stronger one for me. Do you think you could do that for me?"

Velcro gulped down her food. "I..." She looked away awkwardly. "I guess I could."

"It would make me feel a whole lot better about leaving, knowing that at least you two were getting along okay."

"Daddy," Velcro asked timidly.

"Hmm? What is it, precious?"

"How long are you going away for this time?"

"Well, I think this one's going to be a long one. They're sending me to another country-"

"To fight?" Velcro asked.

Her father's eyes widened. Biting his lower lip, he nodded his head. "Yes, precious. To fight."

"But what about the most important lesson you taught me?" Velcro asked. "You said to never use those techniques, not unless you really have to. Daddy, do you *really* have to go away and fight?"

"If I didn't have to," her father said, looking down at the table, "you know I wouldn't, precious."

Velcro observed her father from across the table. Something about the look on his face seemed off. He had a troubled look, as if he's been asking these same questions himself.

The next morning, her father threw his bag over his shoulder. He tried in vain to walk out the door. However, Velcro had her arms wrapped around his leg, and she refused to let loose.

"Come on, don't do that," her father said. "You're acting like a kitten."

"But I *am* a kitten," Velcro mewed.

Her father sighed. "I know you don't want me to leave," he said. "I don't want to go, either. But I need you to be strong for me." Velcro looked up into her father's eyes. He looked down with a loving smile. "And I know you can do it. I've watched you grow so much stronger these past few months."

She let go of his leg, standing up tall.

"Now *that's* my girl," he said, rustling her hair.

"Daddy," Velcro said.

"Yes, precious?"

"I'm gonna keep training while you're gone." She pressed a fist to her chest. "And when you get back, I'll even be stronger than *you*."

"Ha, I can't wait to see it," he laughed.

He smiled down at her one last time, then turned and walked away. Velcro didn't move from that spot, not until he was well out of sight. Once she could no longer see him, though, the tears she was holding back flowed freely to the grass at her feet.

Chapter 20

Keeping her promise, Velcro continued to train by herself at the Twin Trees. She practiced all of the moves she had been taught. But without her father there to guide her, she felt lost. Her sessions grew shorter and shorter as she became less and less motivated.

When she went out to train next, she sat on the bench at the Twin Trees. *'Why am I feeling this way?'* she thought, kicking at the grass. *'I'm never going to catch up to Daddy like this. What's gotten into me?'*

As she sat, staring at the ground, she couldn't help but notice as a small, green lizard crawled by. "Hmm..."

Her eyes suddenly lit up. "Oh, I know!" She hopped off the bench, scaring the lizard away. She punched her fist into her palm, nodding her head with a smirk.

She headed out into the field of tall grass. *'Maybe if I actually put my skills to use, I'll be able to keep going,'* she thought as she scouted out her prey. *'Daddy says I've gotten stronger, but I need to see it for myself.'*

Soon, she found him again. The lizard. She crept forward, the grass barely moving without a rustle. The lizard remained unaware of her presence as he wandered about without a care. Carefully, Velcro reared back, ready to make her move.

She leaped out. Her paws touched down with a thump, kicking up dirt in her eyes. She shook the debris out of her face and looked down at her hands. Lying between her outstretched claws was the lizard.

'*I did it.*' She smiled, giddy.

But as the lizard under her paw was squirming around furiously, trying desperately to get free, Velcro's smile vanished. Watching her helpless victim, her father's words spoke clearly in her head.

"Never use any of these techniques that I've taught you."

"Only use them if absolutely necessary," Velcro finished her father's lesson. She lifted her paw, setting the lizard free. It zoomed deep within the tall grass, running away for its life.

Still, as she watched the reptile run off, Velcro couldn't help but smile. '*Daddy, I really* have *gotten stronger, haven't I?*' She stood up, looking out over the field as the wind blew the grass from side to side. '*But I'm not done yet,*' she thought, taking in a whiff of the cool breeze. '*I'm still gonna get even stronger. Just you wait.*'

Velcro went home later that day. She sat at the table, scribbling away with her tongue sticking out the side of her mouth. She had a new motivation to continue her training. But first, she had an unfinished battle in her drawing book that needed an ending.

"There," she said, dropping her pencil and marveling at her work. She had vanquished her latest opponent. But unlike in times past, she didn't stand alone in her victory. Instead, in this drawing, she had helped her own enemy to his feet. And together they stood, shaking hands after a hard fought battle.

'*I think Daddy would like this,*' she thought, smiling

proudly at her work.

Knock! Knock! Knock!

Velcro turned to the door curiously. '*Who could that be?*' When she opened the door to find out, she was greeted by a tall brown dog. And judging by the dark red dress uniform he wore, he was a senior officer in the Devil Corps.

"Good evening, sweetheart," the Devil greeted. "You must be Velcro."

"Y-yes, sir," Velcro responded nervously.

"Your brother wouldn't happen to be around, would he?"

"N-no. I don't know where he is," she said.

"Oh, that's too bad. I really wanted to tell you both together."

"Tell us what?" Velcro asked.

The Devil sighed. "I'm afraid I have some very unfortunate news." The uniformed Devil frowned, taking in a deep breath. He took off his cover, looking down at the young cat with sorrow in his eyes. "It's about your father."

Velcro bit down on her lower lip, fearing the worst. "Daddy?"

The Devil could only shake his head. "I'm so sorry."

Chapter 21

It was raining at the funeral. And, despite being sheltered from the rain, it was pouring under Velcro's umbrella as well. Her tears streamed down to the sulking grass at her feet. The pelting rain drops drowned out the voice of the chaplain. She peered through her watery eyes, past the black blur of congregators, as her father's casket was lowered into the ground.

'*Daddy...*'

As the ceremony concluded, Velcro finally lifted her head. She looked around her, watching as everyone began to disperse. The ceremony was attended by a handful of Highland's villagers, though the Devil Corps showed the strongest presence.

But she wasn't concerned with any of them right now. She looked all around her, stretching and tilting her neck as she tried to see past all of the adults. But try as she might, she couldn't find the one she was looking for.

"Charlie," she whispered under her breath, standing alone in the rain by her father's resting place.

Later that night, Velcro stepped into the front door of her house. When she turned on the light, she was startled to find that Charlie was home. He was sitting down at the table, his back turned to her.

"You're back already?" He asked.

Velcro pursed her mouth. "Why didn't you go, Charlie?"

"Hmph, what's the point?" he replied.

"What do you mean 'what's the point'? He's our father!"

"Yeah, and he left us," Charlie said. "He left us again. The only difference is, this time, he's not coming back."

Velcro growled under her breath, storming across the room. "How could you say something like that?" she demanded, snatching Charlie by the shoulder. "Why do you always gotta act like such a brat?" She twirled Charlie around to face her, but Charlie shoved her paw away.

"You're such an idiot," Charlie said, standing up out of his chair.

"*Grrr*, would you just shut up, Charlie!"

"Don't you get it," Charlie said, his back still turned to his sister.

"Get *what?*" Velcro snapped.

"Dad's gone, Velcro. He's gone, and he's not coming back," Charlie then turned to face his sister. He looked her in the eyes, though his own remained hidden behind a pair of dark sunglasses. "We're strays now, Velcro."

Velcro widened her gaze, and her jaw began to tremble.

"We can't just play around like a couple of kittens anymore," Charlie continued. "We've got to take care of ourselves now." Charlie threw a backpack over his shoulders, turning towards the door.

"So you're leaving then?" Velcro asked.

"I don't really see the point in sticking around anymore. We'll have a better chance at making it out there."

"But where will you go?" Velcro asked, dipping her eyes to the floor.

"I don't know yet. But I know I don't wanna stay here. So," he turned to his sister, "are you gonna come with me or what?"

Velcro continued to look away, shaking her head. "No. I'm staying."

"Huh? Why?" Charlie demanded. "There's nothing here for you anymore."

"I've got something I still need to do," Velcro replied.

"Like *what?* You're not still thinking about that Devil crap, are you?"

Velcro could only pull her head away.

Charlie grunted. "You should just forget about all that Devil stuff, Velcro. Look where it got Dad."

"No," Velcro replied. "I can't."

"Bah, whatever," Charlie shouted, stomping to the door. "I don't care. Do what you want, idiot."

He paused as he stepped out the door. He looked inside one last time. He let out a sigh as he lowered his head, and he gently shut the door.

With Charlie now gone, Velcro muttered under her breath. *"You're* the idiot."

She continued to stare at the floor, her mind racing. '*I can't,*' she repeated to herself, as tears began to stream down her cheeks. She wiped an arm across her eyes, then lifted her head high. She pressed her fist to her chest. And then, fighting the tears back, she spoke the last words she ever said to her father.

"I'm gonna keep training while you're gone. And when you get back-" she bit her lower lip, losing the fight against her crying eyes. Gritting her teeth, squeezing her eyes shut, she forced the last words out of her mouth. "Then, I'll even be stronger than *you*."

Chapter 22

Velcro continued her training through the years that followed. Day and night, rain or shine, every single day, she went out and practiced. Every day she worked harder than the last. She was determined to keep her word, so she couldn't afford to slack off. She had to become stronger. She had to grow up.

And then came the day she was old enough to enlist. As she was gathering her things at home to set off, she stumbled upon her old drawing book. She picked it up, looking curiously at the cover. '*This old thing. I haven't touched this in years.*'

She took a moment to herself, sitting at the table to look over her past work. Nostalgic memories rushed through her as she relived her old battles. '*I was such a kitten then,*' she chuckled, nodding her head.

Then she turned to the last page, to the last picture she drew in the book. There she stood, holding hands with her defeated foe. Her smile dissolved as she stared at the page. '*No one offered their hand to you, did they?*' She pursed her mouth, crumpling the paper as she tightened her grip on the book. '*No, all they offered you was* death.'

She ripped the picture out. Holding it in her hands,

she stood up and tore it to shreds. She watching in silence as the pieces floated to the floor. She took in a deep breath, then picked up her bag. Leaving her book on the table, and the pieces strewn about, she stepped out the door.

That night, Velcro headed into town. The streets were empty, and the buildings were old and wooden. She walked towards an alley, where Charlie and his friends were hanging out under a streetlamp. He sat on a box with a young, slinky calico cat by his side, playing cards with Rocky and Stan.

Charlie lifted his head as Velcro approached. "Hmm? What're you doing here?"

"I'm leaving," Velcro said.

"So you're really joining the Devil Corps?" Charlie asked.

"Yeah," Velcro responded.

"Huh, whatever." Charlie turned back to his cards. "Wouldn't be the first time I've been abandoned."

Velcro scowled at her brother. *"Charlie."*

"I just don't get you," Charlie continued. "After what happened, why would you still want to join?"

"Because I made a promise. And," she furrowed her eyes, "I have to avenge our father."

Charlie lifted his eyes from his cards. "Vengeance? Really?" He laughed at his sister. "Good god, you're still such a kitten. How are you gonna avenge him, huh? Do you even *know* who killed him? Or are you gonna just go and kill the whole damn country? Will he be 'avenged' then?"

Velcro pulled her face away. "Shut up, Charlie. At least I'm doing something. Are you really content just being some punk stray your whole life?"

"Whatever," Charlie shook his head. "Go on. Go 'avenge' Dad. Go get killed for nothing. You idiot."

Velcro huffed, twirling around and stamping away.

"Hey Charlie," Rocky spoke up. "Who was that, anyways?"

"That's Velcro, my sister. You've met her before, moron."

"*That's* Velcro?" Rocky awed. "Wow, she's beautiful."

Velcro shifted her eyes to the side, overhearing the conversation.

"*What?*" Charlie punched Rocky on the top of his head. "Shut up, Rocky."

Velcro shook her head. '*He's content just goofing off with those fools, and he has the nerve to call* me *a kitten. But I'll show him.*' She turned her eyes to the clear night sky. '*Daddy, I'll make you proud.*'

"Hey, Velcro."

She turned around, and Charlie pounced at her, pinning her down to the ground.

"Dammit, Charlie!"

"You sure you're ready for the Devil Corps?" Charlie laughed.

Velcro shoved Charlie off of her. She stood up, brushing herself off. "Just leave me alone. You're not gonna change my mind."

"No, I know I'm not gonna stop you," Charlie stood up to his feet. "You're gonna do what you're gonna do. But hey, maybe when you get back, you'll actually be able to beat me."

"Hmph," Velcro turned her back. "I'll show you."

Charlie shrugged his shoulders. Without another word, Charlie and Velcro turned their backs to one another. He returned to his group, while she headed towards the village gates. '*I'll show you, Charlie.*'

Chapter 23

"Platoon, atten-*huh!*"

Velcro snapped to attention, as did everyone else in her platoon. There were anxious eyes and trembling knees among the new batch of recruits. But Velcro stood confidently, garbed in her brand new camouflage uniform.

The Drill Sergeant, a growling white dog, marched down the center of the squad bay. She peered from under her large campaign cover, eyeballing her new recruits that stood on either side of her.

"So you all wanna become Devils, huh?"

"Yes, ma'am!" The platoon shouted back weakly.

"Bull. I can't hear you."

"*Yes, ma'am!*"

"That's more like it," she said. "Well I've got news for you. Nobody's gonna just hand you the title of Devil. You're all here because you wanted it, and by all that's holy, you're gonna *earn* it. This isn't going to be a cakewalk. I'm telling you all right now, the road to becoming a Devil is gonna be long and rough, I'll make sure of that. So I hope you all have a really good excuse for trying to join my Corps.

"You!" the Drill Sergeant spat into the face of an unsuspecting recruit. "What's your excuse?"

"Ma'am," the recruit nervously responded. "To serve

my country, ma'am!"

"Psh," the Drill Sergeant shook her head in disappointment. "Typical response. I won't expect much from you."

As she continued down the aisle, her eyes fell on Velcro. "And how about you? What's your name, recruit?"

"Velcro, ma'am!"

"Recruit Velcro, huh?" She shouted in the cat's face. "Well, Recruit Velcro, what's *your* excuse for joining my Corps?"

Velcro replied without skipping a beat, "Revenge, ma'am."

The Drill Sergeant was dumbfounded. "Revenge?" She asked, placing her hands on her hips. "Revenge against whom? Explain yourself, Recruit."

"The enemy, ma'am."

"Huh." The Drill Sergeant nodded her head. "Well, I'm not sure about your reasoning, but I like your attitude, Recruit."

Velcro responded, "Aye, ma'am!"

Later on, the platoon changed over into their physical training gear. The Drill Sergeant rushed them outside, where they prepared to run a marathon under the blazing hot sun. "You better get used to the heat," the Drill Sergeant barked at her panting recruits. "You're gonna be feeling a whole lot of it if you want to be a Devil." Most of the platoon was slogging along, their tongues flailing out of their wide open mouths. "You think this is hot?" The Drill Sergeant screamed. "Just wait till you make it to Hell!"

Velcro remained strong, though, running towards the front of the pack. Taking steady breaths, she tossed the drench out of her eyes, pushing through with utmost determination.

"Hey," a recruit by her side spoke aloud. Velcro tried to ignore her, but she persisted. "Hey girl, you're name's Velcro, right?"

"Uh, right," Velcro responded, looking over from the corner of her eye.

"Hey, I'm Honey," the recruit continued through heavy breaths. She was a gorgeous, busty calico cat. Running beside Velcro, she resembled a model more than a soldier. And compared to the rest of the platoon, she was clearly in decent shape.

"That was kinda weird what you said before," Honey continued.

"What was?" Velcro asked.

"About joining out of revenge. And you seem pretty serious about it, too. So you're gonna fill me in on what that's all about, right?"

Velcro pulled her eyes forward. "Just concentrate on your running. You're slowing us both down."

"Oh fine, don't wanna tell me, huh?" Honey teased.

"Hey you two!" Velcro and Honey snapped their necks straight at the sound of their Drill Sergeant's voice. "We must not be moving fast enough if you've still got the strength to talk. Good, *double time*."

"Aye, ma'am!" Velcro and Honey shouted together. They instantly picked up their pace, the Drill Sergeant right on their backs.

"Let's go, hurry up," the Drill Sergeant shouted. "Hup-two, hup-two, move it!"

That night, after lights went out, Velcro lay in her bed. Resting her arms under her head, she stared up at the bottom of the bunk above her. *Everyone keeps questioning my* motives,' she thought. '*I thought Charlie was just messing with me, but even the Drill Sergeant...*' Velcro turned over to the rack beside her, where Honey had already fallen fast asleep. '*And her, too. Do my reasons really not make any sense?*

'*Maybe Charlie* was *right. I mean, after all, how* do *I determine whether or not Daddy's been avenged? I don't even know who killed him. It was just another soldier in another country who was just doing his duty.*

'*So, what* does *it mean to avenge my father?*' As Velcro lay there, questioning her own motives, her mind could only draw a blank. She didn't have any answers.

Chapter 24

The various platoons had all gathered around under a large canopy. They sat on the mulch surrounding the wooden stage on which their Drill Sergeants stood. A lean, fit orange cat sporting a tight black shirt stood at the head of the instructors. He turned his head from side to side, observing the recruits before him. "Good morning, recruits."

"Good morning, sir!" The company responded.

"Today, we'll be going over hand to hand combat."

A smirk formed on Velcro's face. *'Yes. I've been waiting for this.'*

"Drill Sergeant," the orange cat shouted behind him. "Could you please help me demonstrate this first attack?"

Velcro watched as her platoon's Drill Sergeant stepped forward. Velcro tried her best to pay close attention, but something brushing against the back of her head distracted her. She remained still, trying to keep her composure. As the brushing continued, though, her ears flickered, and her eyebrows furrowed.

And then she snapped.

She reached behind her, smacking whatever it was that had been brushing her head. Feeling something furry within her palm, she looked behind to investigate. She had latched onto a bushy tail. And it belonged to none other than

Honey, who just so happened to be sitting beside her.

"Hey girl, what're you grabbin' my tail for?" Honey whispered, tugging her tail out of Velcro's hand.

"Watch where you wag that thing," Velcro hissed back. Velcro shook her head, turning back to the demonstration. Out of the corner of her eye, she could see Honey fumbling about with something. She chanced a glance at the calico, and was astonished by what she found.

Honey was looking into a pocket mirror. Licking the fur on her paws, she had been grooming herself this whole time. "Hey," Velcro whispered, "don't you think you should put that away and pay attention?"

"Huh, oh this?" Honey said, smiling into her mirror. "Sweety, us girls gotta take advantage of this downtime we have to look our best."

'*Downtime?*' Velcro was insulted.

"And besides," Honey continued, "I already know all of this stuff, so I'm good. After all, I *did* score the highest out of anyone in the entrance exams."

'*She* what?' Velcro let out a huff. '*I don't believe that for a second. Not her.*'

Honey looked over at Velcro, a cocky grin on her face. "What, you're not jealous, are you? If you're *really* worried about learning this stuff, maybe I can show you a thing or two back at the barracks."

'*Is she for real?*' Velcro wondered, cocking an eyebrow. '*She's not taking this seriously at all, and she wants to show* me *a thing or two?*'

Honey threw her head back, looking back into her mirror. "Of course, if I were willing to open up and help you out, I'd want you to open up a little to me in return. You know what I mean?"

"Hmph," Velcro snapped her head forward. "Who

says I need your help?"

"*You two!*"

Both Velcro's and Honey's eyes widened as the instructors on stage pointed out to them. '*Crap, not again.*'

"Perhaps you two would like to come up here and demonstrate what we've just shown you," the orange cat yelled out.

"Aye, sir," the two cats stood to their feet. Honey snapped her mirror shut, putting it away as they approached the wooden stage.

'*This is the second time she's gotten me in trouble,*' Velcro growled. '*But that's okay. Now's my chance to show* her *a thing or two.*'

The two climbed onto the stage, where they stood staring face to face. The instructors took a step back, watching on with their hands on their hips.

"Since you two were paying *so* much attention," the orange cat mocked, "I want to see you two utilize what we've shown you to try and take each other down."

"How about we make a deal," Honey suggested to Velcro.

"Just shut up," Velcro insisted, "we're in enough trouble as it is."

"If I beat you, you have to fess up about your whole revenge thing."

"Honey-"

"But if you beat me," Honey interrupted, "then I'll still be willing to help you out, but I won't bother you anymore, if that's what you want."

"Enough talking," their Drill Sergeant barked.

"Aye, ma'am," Honey responded.

"Well I'm waiting," the Drill Sergeant continued.

Velcro and Honey grabbed out at one another. They

latched onto the other's neck and elbow, pulling each other in.
"So, do we have a deal?" Honey persisted.

"If I say yes, will you shut up already?" Velcro sneered.

"Heh, if that's what you want."

"Then *yes*." Velcro shoved Honey back.

She threw a punch, which Honey blocked. She kicked up at Honey's face, but Honey caught her foot.

Honey pushed Velcro onto her back. She stomped down, but Velcro rolled out of harm's way. Velcro swept at Honey's legs, but the calico jumped over.

Velcro stood back up. She threw out a series of chops, all of which Honey managed to dodge. '*She's tougher than I thought.*'

Honey blocked the last chop. She threw a punch, but Velcro swiped it away, sending Honey off balance.

Velcro moved in for a decisive blow, but Honey ducked. She lifted Velcro up over her head, sending the brown tabby landing flat on her back.

'*Damn, I can't believe this,*' Velcro thought, cringing from the brunt of the fall. As she looked up through squinted eyes, she saw that Honey had turned her back. She was gloating to her fellow recruits who were cheering her on. '*Now's my chance,*' Velcro thought, rolling onto her stomach.

She reached out, grabbing Honey by the ankle.

"What the-"

Velcro snatched back, planting Honey chest first to the stage. Velcro leaped on top of her, locking her arms behind her back as she pressed Honey's face to the ground.

"You're better than I expected," Velcro smirked.

"Heh," Honey chuckled. "Same to you."

"That's enough," the orange cat shouted, pulling Velcro off. "Now, I don't know where you two learned all of

110

that, but that was *not* what we had just demonstrated up here."

"Aye, sir," Velcro said, watching as Honey climbed back to her feet.

"Now the two of you, go back to your seats and *pay attention*," he shouted.

"Aye, sir!" Both Velcro and Honey rushed off the stage in a pant.

"Oh, and one more thing, you two," the orange cat continued. Velcro and Honey turned around to see the instructor had a huge grin on his face. "Good job, recruits."

Velcro and Honey snapped to attention. *"Aye, sir!"* They used what energy they had left to hide their excitement. They were brimming with motivation.

Chapter 25

That night, when the platoon was granted a brief free time, Honey approached Velcro, who was sitting on her foot-locker. "Well, you beat me," Honey said with a shrug, "so I guess I'll leave you alone now." Honey turned away, waving her bushy tail behind her as she headed towards the litter.

"Wait," Velcro said. "I actually *did* want to talk to you about something."

"Oh?" Honey looked over her shoulder. "What about?"

"It's about my motives," Velcro continued.

"So you're really gonna fill me in?" Honey pranced over to Velcro, sitting on the locker beside her. "No more of this brooding quiet act?"

"Well, not exactly," Velcro responded. "I was just wondering, why do you want to know about me so badly? Are my reasons really *that* out of the ordinary?"

"Hmm, well, I don't suppose you'd accept curiosity as an appropriate answer?" Honey mused.

"If you said that, I'd ask if you ever heard how curiosity killed the cat." Velcro smirked, showing off her claws in jest.

"Sweety, you're crazy," Honey laughed. "But seriously, there's something different about you."

Velcro raised an eyebrow. "What do you mean?"

"I mean, you're not like the rest of the recruits here. I could see it myself from the get go, the way you carry yourself, you're much more driven than anyone else here. I mean, even the Drill Sergeant's noticed it. So that's why, when you told us why you're doing this, it just intrigued me." Honey leaned back, placing her paws on the back of her head. "Revenge, huh? I guess you just don't hear about that too often outside of story books and such."

"Well, to be honest with you," Velcro began, "I didn't think too highly of you at first."

"No kidding?" Honey rolled her eyes.

"Well, the thing is, you've shown me that you're clearly a step ahead of everyone else here already. But the way you carry *yourself*, it's almost like you just don't care."

"Huh, is that so?" Honey sat up straight. "Well, I guess I've just been preparin' for this whole military thing for so long, that now that I'm here, it kinda just feels a little like home. I don't have to be a mindless drone, I'm okay still being myself. Just so long as I can do my job in the end, right?"

Velcro nodded her head, looking to the floor as she listened on.

"It's like I said today," Honey continued. "When I told you that we gotta use our downtime to look our best. I could tell you took offense to that remark. But what I meant was, we're about to become Devils. That means that there's a whole lotta people who are gonna be looking up to us. We're going to be role models, Velcro. And, while it's certainly important to be able to fight and defend our country, it's equally as important to look the part, too. Take you, for instance."

"What about me?" Velcro shifted her glaring eyes back to Honey.

"Well," Honey smiled, "lets just say that the whole tomcat look ain't exactly doing you any favors, sweety."

Velcro sneered at the comment. "What're you trying to say?"

"Oh you know... hey!" Honey's eyes brightened. "Why don't I give you a makeover?"

"Uh, no thanks," Velcro shied away.

"Oh come on, it'll be fun."

"I said *no*," Velcro growled.

"Okay, okay," Honey held up her hands. "No need to get all worked up, sweety."

"Though, I can see your point," Velcro steered back on topic. "About looking the part. I guess I never really thought about that. All this time I've just been focused on the physical part, but you're right. We *are* gonna be role models, aren't we?"

"That's right, girl," Honey nodded her head. "We've gotta show 'em that not just anybody can be a Devil. It takes something special. And we've gotta show that to 'em even when we're not out on the battlefield."

Velcro looked Honey over. She was sitting with her hands grabbing the locker, kicking her feet in the air as she lifted her head high. She really was unlike all the rest. She was concerned with her appearance, but there was so much more to her. She was strong, both physically and mentally. And even more than that, she was smart. *'And here I was thinking she wasn't taking this seriously,'* Velcro snickered. *'But still...'*

"There's just one thing I don't get," Velcro said.

"Hmm?" Honey turned to Velcro. "What's that?"

"Why did *you* join the Devil Corps?"

"Oh, well that's an easy one. I grew up in a military family, so I've been exposed to the lifestyle my whole life."

Honey smiled brightly. "It just felt like the natural progression for me, I guess."

Velcro was taken aback by her response. "Who in your family was in the Corps?"

"Both of my parents were Devils. And they actually met each other in the Devil Corps. They both joined to serve their country, and in return for their service, they each found true love. How romantic is that?" Honey clasped her hands together, staring out into space with glowing eyes. "Who knows, maybe you and I will find true love here, too. Wouldn't that be lovely?"

"Yeah," Velcro sighed, dipping her head. "Lovely. So then your parents are both still around?"

"Huh?" The dancing hearts fluttering about in Honey's head had popped. "Yeah, of course they are. Why wouldn't they be?"

Velcro shook her head. "It's nothing."

Honey shrugged her shoulders, smiling brightly. Velcro stared at the calico with wondrous eyes, her mouth cracked open in awe. And seeing the genuine bliss on Honey's face, Velcro couldn't help but smile back.

* * *

"She reminded me of my old self," Velcro said to Maggie, her arms wrapped around her legs as she sat in the corner of her grim prison cell. "The way she talked, the way she carried herself, it reminded me of why I originally wanted to join the Devil Corps. And seeing how happy she was, it made me want to go back to those times. And so I decided, then and there, to return to my original goal. I wasn't doing it out of revenge anymore. From that point on, I was doing it to be the best."

Velcro bobbed her head, taking a moment to gather her thoughts. "For the next few years, things went smoothly. I was promoted fast, and placed in charge of my own troops. I hadn't heard from Honey since we graduated basic, but then one day, I was granted the chance to see her again. She was stationed at the base where I was to receive my next orders."

Velcro furrowed her brows. "That was the day that everything changed, though." There was fire in her eyes as she spoke her hate filled words. "It was the day I met *him*."

CHAPTER 26

Velcro walked through the forest, heading towards the main headquarters of the Devil Corps, a building known as The Hexagon, where she was to receive her latest orders. She was bobbing her head, humming a cheery tune. But as she strolled on, another loud hum overthrew her music. She stopped, looking up into the trees, in the direction of the sound.

"Oh wow," she gasped, staring at the largest beehive she had ever laid eyes on. At about a third the size of the tree, it dwarfed the branch that it hang from. Buzzing bees were swarming all around, and a sticky orange substance was oozing, dripping down to Velcro's feet.

"Hmm," Velcro pondered at the honey on the ground. "I heard *she's* been stationed here. It *has* been a while." Velcro smiled, looking ahead towards her destination. "I should try and see if I can't squeeze in a quick visit while I'm there." Velcro pushed forward, running the remainder of the way to the base.

As she made it to the forest outskirts, she stopped, placing her hands on her knees in a pant. The sun was setting in the distance, stretching The Hexagon's shadows out to the forest. Velcro stared out at the massive building before her, the reddened sky illuminating as its backdrop.

She approached the Southwest end, one of six sides that made up the building's shapely structure. As she wandered through the building's halls, she stopped a passerby to ask about her friend's whereabouts.

"Yeah, she's probably in her office," the helpful dog responded, giving Velcro the directions to get there. Velcro nodded with a smile, and she was off on her way.

She lived out fond memories in her head, of the two sparring with one another to hone their fighting skills, and even helping out their peers after they had gained notoriety with their impressive match. *'It'll be great to see her again. I wonder how much stronger she's gotten since those days.'*

Velcro stopped in front of her door inscribed 'Lt. Honey'. *'Lieutenant, huh?'* Velcro raised an eyebrow. She shrugged her shoulders, knocking on the door.

"Come on in," she heard the familiar voice. Velcro creaked the door open, peering in to see Honey sitting behind a desk. "Huh?" Honey lifted her head. "Who's that? Is that-?"

"It's been a while," Velcro said with a smile.

"Velcro!" Honey's eyes lit up. "What're you doin' here, girl?"

"I'm here to receive my orders," Velcro stood in front of the desk. "Figured I'd pay you a visit while I'm here."

"Wow, I did not expect you strollin' on in here," Honey shook her head in delight. "You're looking great."

"Thanks," Velcro said. She crossed her arms, rocking on her heels as Honey remained seated behind her desk. "Oh, and don't bother getting up or anything," Velcro teased with a smirk.

"Ha!" Honey mocked with a smirk of her own. But then her smile washed away from her face. "Oh, wait. That's right, you don't know, do you?"

Velcro tilted her head. "Know what?"

Velcro's jaw dipped. Her eyes widened as Honey made her way around her desk. The once athletically agile beauty remained seated, now confined to a wheelchair.

Honey let out a sigh, shrugging her shoulders in response to Velcro's look of shock. "You don't have to say anything, sweety."

"But..." Velcro struggled to find the words. "How? What happened?"

"Combat wound," Honey said simply. "And yeah, I know it sucks. But enough about that. I'm tired of talking about my injuries. Dwelling on it just makes things seem worse than they are, right?"

"Honey..."

"But hey, it's not all bad," Honey forced a smile. "After my injury, the Corps wasn't sure what to do with me. They probably would've just discharged me, if not for my high test scores. It seems they still had some use for me, and so they relocated me here."

"Use for you?" Velcro asked, still visibly shaken.

"Yeah." Honey pressed a thumb to her chest. "I'm a part of the High Counsel now."

"What?" Velcro's arms dropped to her sides. "Really? The High Counsel? How did you manage that?"

"I dunno," Honey shrugged. "I guess someone with my smarts and combat experience was a valuable asset to them."

"Huh," Velcro placed her hands on her hips, tapping her foot. "I'm supposed to go before the High Counsel tomorrow to receive my orders." Velcro shook her head, chuckling to herself.

"And...?" Honey awaited a response. "What's so funny about that?"

"Oh, it's nothing," Velcro said. "I just never thought

I'd see the day when I'd be getting ordered around by *you*."

Honey playfully sneered her face. "Hmph. Is that so, huh?" She laughed it off herself. "Well, I actually won't be present for your mission briefing tomorrow."

"And why's that?" Velcro questioned.

"Well, I'm still new at this sort of thing, and I *am* the junior member. So I guess they're willing to hear what I have to say, but they don't trust me enough yet to actually give out the orders myself."

"Oh, well that's too bad."

The two exchanged silence for a brief moment. Velcro's heart had sunk when she first saw Honey in a wheelchair. But seeing how happy Honey appeared despite her new physical shortcomings, Velcro was reminded of why they became friends in the first place. And she couldn't help but smile back warmly.

The next day, Velcro sat patiently, waiting just outside of the High Counsel's briefing room.

'I wonder why they had me come here *to get my orders,'* Velcro thought. *'Whatever it is, it must be pretty important. I've never gone before the High Counsel before.'*

The door swung open, and a short brown dachshund stuck his head out. "Velcro?"

"Yes, sir," Velcro stood up.

"The High Counsel will now see you."

Velcro followed the small dog into the vast, dark red room. On the wall before her stood five pillars. An officer of the Devil Corps was perched on all but the far left pillar, which remained empty.

The center pillar stood taller than the rest. Atop this one was a General, as signified by the four shining stars he wore on the collar of his dress uniform. He was a large,

120

brown, musclebound pit bull. He smiled ferociously, glaring down at Velcro, who stood at the center of the room.

"So *you're* Velcro," the General spoke, his deep voice booming.

"Yes, sir," Velcro responded in her normal tone, standing at ease with her hands behind her back.

"Speak up," the dachshund barked. "Don't you realize who that is you're talking to?"

The General waved his hand. "Enough."

The short dog snapped to attention. "Aye, sir." He took a step back, twirling around, then stepped out of the room, slamming the door shut behind him.

The large canine grinned. He clasped his palms together, placing them on the railing before him. "It's a pleasure to finally meet you, Velcro. Before we get down to business, I'd like to properly introduce myself."

Velcro gulped. Standing before this audience put her spirit to the test. The mere presence of the General intimidated her to her very core. '... *Why?*' Despite all of her years of discipline, it took everything she had to keep her composure and stand still. '*Why am I feeling this way?*'

The General showed off his fangs with delight. "I'm certain you've heard of me." His eyes flared as he spoke his name. "I am the *Devil Dog.*"

Chapter 27

"I am the *Devil Dog*." His booming voice sent shivers through Velcro's fur. The General grinned with his fangs in plain sight. "Tell me, Velcro, do you have any idea as to why I summoned you here?"

"No, sir, I don't," Velcro responded.

"Good," he said, "because what I'm about to tell you is top secret. This information absolutely cannot be leaked. And we will prevent such a leak, at any cost. Do you understand me?"

"Yes, sir," Velcro said.

"Are you positive?" The Devil Dog eyeballed the cat. "Are you absolutely certain that you understand the severity of my claims?"

Velcro looked straight into the eyes of the Devil Dog, responding with a firm, confident stance. "*Yes*, sir."

"Good." The Devil Dog leaned back in his chair. "In that case, this is your mission. You are to infiltrate the village of Bugleville."

'*Bugleville?*' Velcro thought, furrowing her brows. '*Isn't that one of our own villages? What could be going on there?*'

"You will be accompanied by a small squad," the General continued, "all of whom have been hand picked by me personally. They've all already been briefed on the mission. They're currently on stand-by, waiting for their Squad Leader. Velcro," he leaned forward, "I want *you* to be that Squad Leader."

"After we enter Bugleville," Velcro asked, "what are you going to have us do?"

"Straight to the point, eh?" The Devil Dog snickered. "Okay then, this is your objective. There's a reason why I asked for you specifically to take charge of this mission. Do you have any idea as to what that reason may be?"

"No, sir," Velcro shook her head, pursing her mouth.

"To put it simply, you're one of the best we've got. In some ways, you could say that it's been *years* since I've seen someone as skilled as you among our ranks in the Devil Corps. So if there's anyone who can achieve success in this mission, it would definitely be you, Velcro."

'*Just what* is *this mission?*' Velcro was growing anxious.

"Once you've successfully infiltrated Bugeville," the General continued, "your mission will proceed as follows."

Velcro's eyes widened as the General issued her orders.

"You'll start by creating mass confusion within the village. Utilizing your squad, you are to create a perimeter. Attacking it from the shadows on all fronts, you will create the illusion that the village is being attacked by a force much larger than the one we're sending in."

Velcro's ears twitched. She shook her head. "Excuse me?"

"*Then,*" the General moved forward with the briefing, "you will proceed to overwhelm the village. Take as many lives as necessary, and *force* the village into absolute submission. When Bugleville is at your mercy, you will round up all who remain and take them prisoner. Kill anyone who shows any signs of restraint. Anyone who fails to cooperate

123

must be *put down*."

Velcro's fists were trembling behind her back. "What is this?" Velcro spat out her words through clenched fangs. "Is this some kind of sick *joke?*"

"No," the General responded, "this is no joke. And that's precisely why we need you for this mission, Velcro."

"Why?" Velcro glared at the General, her tail whipping wildly. *"Why?* What purpose could there possibly be for attacking our own people?"

"You don't need to know the specifics," the Devil Dog replied. "It's irrelevant to the mission."

"If there's a threat within the village," Velcro retorted, "we should focus on the threat alone and leave the innocent civilians out of it. How could you even consider slaughtering an entire village?"

"You do *not* need to know that," the General repeated. "That information is *irrelevant*."

"Oh, I think that information is *very* relevant," Velcro disagreed.

The officer to the Devil Dog's right spoke up. "You are *through* talking back to the General."

The Devil Dog lifted a hand to the officer, motioning him to keep calm. "Velcro," the General spoke in a collected tone. "Your lack of obedience is beginning to disappoint me. Perhaps you weren't the right choice for this mission after all."

"Well that's just fine," Velcro fired back, "because I *refuse* to accept such despicable orders."

"Velcro-"

"And not only that," she cut the General off, "but I won't allow anyone else to relieve me of these orders, either. I don't care if this *is* supposed to be top secret."

"Velcro!" the Devil Dog barked. Silenced, Velcro

glared with fiery eyes at the General. The Devil Dog smiled, chuckling to himself as he leaned back in his chair. "Heh, you know, you really are a lot like *him*."

'*Him?*' Velcro's lips parted, and she raised a brow.

"Yes," the Devil Dog gleamed. "You truly are your father's daughter."

Velcro's eyes widened, her brows dipped low. "What did you just say?" She scowled at the General.

"Heh, your father. I remember the day I summoned him before me. I briefed him for a very similar mission. Like you, he was very skilled at what he did." The Devil Dog then closed his eyes, shaking his head in disappointment. "Also like you, he had a complete lack of obedience. Such a shame. He could have been such a valuable asset, if only he were a good, obedient Devil."

"What are you saying?" Velcro demanded he explain himself.

"What I'm saying, Velcro, is this. Should you continue to act belligerently, then you will leave me no choice." The Devil Dog leaned in and let out a huff. "If you refuse these orders, then you will share your father's fate."

"My father?" Velcro lowered her head, her jaw dropped in disbelief. "My father died in combat."

"No," the Devil Dog growled. "He didn't. He died right here, right where you stand." Velcro gritted her teeth. Her heart sank into her stomach as the Devil Dog finished his confession. "Your father died at *my* hands!"

Chapter 28

Velcro lifted her eyes to her father's self-admitted killer. Her fists clenched, her tail twitching, the very fur on her body stood on it's end. She lifted her eyes with a killing gaze at the General Devil Dog.

"You *bastard!*"

The Devil Dog smirked. "Now, are you ready to be a good, obedient Devil, Velcro? Or am I going to have to put you down as well?"

Velcro reached behind her. *'He's the one.'* She sprang up to the Devil Dog's pillar. *'The reason I joined the Corps.'* Staring face to face, she pulled out a dagger, pressing it to the dog's neck. *'The object of my revenge.'*

Even with a blade to his throat, the Devil Dog continued to smile. "Do you really think that *toy* will be enough to kill me?"

"You killed my father," Velcro spat. "I *will* kill you."

"Heh," the General chuckled, "if you say so." Velcro lifted her head to the sounds of rumbling feet approaching from behind the General. "Well I'm waiting," the Devil Dog gloated.

Velcro took one last glare into the eyes of the man who murdered her father. Then right before a squad of Devils surrounded the scene, she flipped backwards off the pillar.

The Devils took aim with their crossbows, but Velcro turned tail, scrambling to the door. She burst out of the room, just avoiding the onslaught of arrows.

"She knows far too much about what we're doing," the General said aloud to his troops. He pointed down to the door, his fingers extended in a knife hand. "Do not let her get away." The Devils hopped off of the pillars, making chase after Velcro.

As Velcro ran through the halls, a siren sounded, and a loud voice spoke over the intercom system. "ATTENTION! THERE IS A FUGITIVE ON THE LOOSE IN THE BUILDING! I REPEAT, THERE IS A FUGITIVE ON THE LOOSE IN THE BUILDING! PLEASE STAY ON ALERT!"

'Great, I'm a fugitive now?' Velcro shook her head, huffing through her nose as she ran.

An arrow whizzed past her head. She looked over her shoulder at the approaching Devils. *'Damn, what have I gotten myself into?'*

She dropped down, grabbing a handful of throwing stars strapped to her ankle. She then twirled to face her oncomers. Leaping into the intersecting hallway, she tossed her stars in the Devils' direction. She rolled to her feet, charging forward full steam. She turned a corner, and then another, until she was certain that she had lost the Devils.

As she ran down the last hall, she passed by the door to Honey's office. She skidded to a halt, looking behind her, listening out for the squad of Devils. Hearing nothing, she proceeded to knock on Honey's door.

"Honey," she whispered, "Honey, are you in there?" She turned the knob, and the door squeaked open. "Honey?" Velcro pushed the door open, but the office was empty. She stepped inside, walking around to the seat of Honey's desk.

'Just how much of this mess are you aware of, Honey?' she

127

thought, staring down at the wooden desk. '*I just can't believe that you'd have any part of this. But...*' Velcro pulled a sheet of paper out of the cabinet. She pressed it down with her palm, frantically scribbling out a quick note.

Velcro's ear twitched as the sounds of storming feet resumed in the hallway. She pulled out her knife, stabbing the note to the desk.

MIDNIGHT.   BEEHIVE.   SOUTHWEST.   COME ALONE.

-V

She rushed over to the door. She peered outside, checking to see that the coast was clear. She then slammed the door behind her, continuing in her escape of The Hexagon.

Midnight came. Hiding within the trees, Velcro waited patiently for Honey to arrive. '*This is stupid,*' she thought, looking up to the moon in the night sky. '*Maybe I shouldn't have left that message. What if she really* is *aware of everything? If so, then I just set myself up to be captured.*'

She looked to the ground, at the massive beehive that hang from the adjacent tree. '*The longer I stick around, the less my chances of escaping become. Come on, Honey. What's taking you?*'

She heard a crackling approaching. Velcro shot her head to the sound, her breath stuck in her chest. As her friend came into sight, rolling across the grass and leaves in her wheelchair, she let out a very relieved sigh.

Honey approached the beehive, staring up curiously at it. "Velcro?" She whispered, looking from side to side.

"Pst," Velcro whispered back.

"Velcro?" Honey looked up into Velcro's tree. "Velcro, is that you?"

"Did anyone follow you?" Velcro asked.

128

"No, no I don't think so," she said. "Just what the heck is going on, Velcro?"

Velcro hopped out of the tree, landing with a crouch. She stood up, staring down at Honey with unsure eyes. "You said that they haven't been letting you in during the mission briefings. But what *are* they letting you in on? Tell me, tell me everything you know, Honey."

"Whoa, slow down, sweety." Honey held up her hands. "What're you talkin' about?"

"I'm talking about the mission that General Devil Dog just gave me." Velcro scrunched her mouth at the mentioning of the General's name. "Does the complete massacre of Bugleville mean anything to you?"

"Massacre?" Honey's eyes widened. "What massacre?"

"You tell me," Velcro said.

"I don't know about any massacre at Bugleville."

"Then what *do* you know?" Velcro snapped. "What kind of things do they talk about when you're present?"

"Well I don't know, girl," Honey shook her head. "They mainly just get my advice on strategies and that sorta thing, and then they dismiss me. They don't let me sit in while they discuss the actual mission details just yet. They're still trying to feel me out, I think." Honey gulped. "Are you really trying to tell me that they've ordered you to massacre the entire village of Bugleville?"

"That's exactly what I'm trying to tell you," Velcro replied.

"But why?"

"That's what I want to know," Velcro crossed her arms, staring down at her feet. "Honey, I need to know that I can trust you."

"Trust me?"

"Yes." Velcro lifted her head, staring Honey in the eyes with a serious expression. "Honey, the Devil Corps is up to something big, and I'm gonna need your help getting to the bottom of it. But I need to know that I can trust you." The two stared in silence at one another, as a cool breeze passed by. "So, can I?"

"Velcro..." Honey lowered her head, taking in a deep breath. "What could I do to help? What do you expect me to do, Velcro?"

"You're on the High Council," Velcro replied. "They don't trust you yet. But you're just going to have to *earn* their trust. Do whatever you can to find out what they're planning."

"What do *you* think they're planning?" Honey asked. "If they ordered the massacre of Bugleville, there's got to be a good reason for it."

"I thought the same thing at first," Velcro said. "But they don't want us to just single out a particular threat within the village. They want to exterminate every single person who lives there, period. And I don't know about you, but I haven't heard of any kind of strange activities going on in Bugleville."

"Me neither," Honey added. "But then, why make such an order?"

"Maybe," Velcro's eyes dipped, "if they're willing to attack one village like this, what's stopping them from doing the same to others?"

"What are you trying to say?" Honey asked. "Are you really suggesting that the Devil Corps intends to wipe out our own country, one by one?"

"I don't know," Velcro huffed. "God I hope not. But the General did mention *something*." Velcro shifted her eyes away. "Something that would suggest that this isn't the first time they've attempted a mission like this. But I just can't-" She paused, returning her gaze to the bewildered calico. "I can't be too sure. And that's why I need your help. I need you to find out the Devil Corps' true intentions. If they *are* planning more attacks, I need to know where, and when. I need to know everything, anything that you can get from them." Velcro glared at Honey, her eyes ablaze with hatred. "Anything that I can use to put a stop to them."

"Velcro..." Honey lost her voice, staring into the fiery eyes of the brown tabby. "I-I'll try my best. I'll do what I can. But what about you?"

"What do you mean?" Velcro asked.

"I mean, what are you gonna do now, sweety? You're a fugitive, you can't exactly just go back to base and rally up the troops. They're gonna lock you away the moment you set foot on military ground."

Velcro nodded her head. "I'm well aware of that, and I'm still working on that. But for the meantime, I'll just have to stay hidden."

"And one more thing," Honey continued, "we can't be meeting up like this again after tonight. It's just too dangerous now, for both me and you. So how will I get a hold of you, assuming I can get that information?"

Velcro looked to the giant beehive. She lifted her arm, pointing at the massive, buzzing hive. "We'll use *them*."

"Them?" Honey tilted her head.

"Oh come on," Velcro said, "someone as smart as you should know of the old bee method of delivering secret messages."

"Oh," Honey nodded, staring up at the beehive herself. "Oh wow, that method's pretty archaic. I'm actually a little surprised you even know about it."

Velcro turned her head away. "My *father* showed it to

131

me."

Honey turned back to her friend with worried eyes. "Velcro-"

"And even if it is old fashioned," Velcro continued, slipping off her cammy top, "it'll be the safest way to communicate for now." She balled up her blouse and tossed it over to Honey. "You can use this. I know *I* won't be needing it much anymore."

Honey clasped the blouse in her palms, biting down on her lower lip.

"Send word as soon as you find anything out." Velcro turned her back to the wheelchaired calico. Looking over her shoulder one last time, she said her parting words. "I'm putting my faith in you, Honey."

She ran off, leaving Honey to watch on as she disappeared into the night. Honey looked down at Velcro's blouse, and she let out a sigh. "Velcro," she whispered to herself. "Good luck."

Chapter 29

"But that was the day that I got my answer," Velcro spoke to Maggie, sitting in her gloomy cell. "When I said that I joined the Corps out of revenge, now I finally knew what it meant. In order to avenge my father, I had to *kill* the Devil Dog."

"Mm," Maggie acknowledged, the first sound she had made in some time. "That was a clever trick, that old bee method."

"Yeah," Velcro said. "I gave her my blouse to use as a tracker. By writing her message on it using honey, the bees would cling to it, taking the form of the message as a collective unit, memorizing it. Then, using my scent left on the blouse, they'd be able to track me down, wherever I was, and deliver the message to me, taking the form of the message and spelling it out in honey for me.

"It's an old method of communication, but it's generally viewed as being too unreliable, so it's been mainly abandoned in recent times. But I wasn't left with too many other, more reliable options. So I was forced to resort to this supposedly 'archaic' method.

"I moved out to Bugleville," Velcro continued. "I couldn't just barge in there as I was, though. I was a wanted fugitive now. I had to disguise myself. And so, I dressed myself in black, hid myself in the shadows. And when I got to Bugleville, I waited patiently on the outskirts, waited for any sign of military movement.

"But nothing happened." Velcro shook her head. "I guess they canceled the attack on that village, now that I knew all about it. But while I was waiting out there, my first message arrived. It was a list of villages that the Devils intended to attack. Sure enough, Bugleville was no longer on the list. And not only that, but the villages they were attacking were much smaller ones.

"So I headed out, starting off the top of the list. The first two were Avonville and Daleville. Easy enough to hit, since they were nearby one another. The numbers sent to these villages were small, with units of around two to four people at the most. I took them out from the shadows, attacking them in the same manner they intended to attack the villages.

"Apparently I wasn't hidden well enough, however. As I walked around town in my spare time, I heard the rumors rummaging about. Of the ghost in the forest, the 'ninja cat' who was attacking our nation's military." Velcro rolled her eyes. "It wasn't just the military personnel talking, either. There were a number of people who claimed to have caught me in the act.

"So naturally, they branded me a terrorist, a foreign spy of some sort. They didn't know what I was after, but they knew that I was attacking the Devil Corps, and that was enough to make me the bad guy."

Velcro shrugged her shoulders. "Along with the false rumors came the confusion of my identity. Most notably, my gender. I didn't mind that people thought that I was a man, however. All that did was make it harder for the Devil Corps to peg me down. I'm sure they had an idea as to who the

Ninja Kat really was, but they didn't have any way to prove it.

"And that's what I did for the following months. I'd wait for Honey's messages, then I'd go down the list. This worked out for some time, but I always knew that this was only a delaying tactic. I'd have to do more eventually if I wanted to really stop the Devils."

Velcro took in a deep breath. She shifted her head to the side, slowly letting the air sift through her nose. "But after some time, the messages quit coming. I didn't think the Devil Corps would just up and stop their attempts just like that. And even if that was the case, why wouldn't Honey communicate that to me?

"I figured something must have happened. I figured Honey must have been caught." Velcro shook her head. "So, against my better judgment, I went back. I just had to know. I had to know what happened to Honey."

Chapter 30

Garbed in her black Ninja Kat outfit, Velcro arrived back at the massive beehive. The bees were still buzzing about, and nothing looked out of the ordinary in the vicinity. *'Honey,'* she thought, staring down at the ground. She tilted her head, *'Hmm, no wheel tracks.'* She looked out in the distance, staring to the Northeast, where The Hexagon lie ahead.

She traveled to the outskirts. She waited in the trees, watching as personnel walked in and out of the building. As the hours trickled on, the sun began to set, and the outer lights turned on. And as the night continued to drag, she found herself fighting to keep her eyelids open.

'Come on, Honey,' she thought, still no sign of her friend. *'You've gotta go home sometime, right?'*

Then Velcro's eyes lit up. There she was. Rolling out the door, Honey glided down the handicap ramp aboard her wheelchair. As she made it to the bottom, a flying object halted her movement. She stared at the dark thing that struck the ground before her. It was a throwing star. And it was dripping with an odd, sticky substance.

"Is that..." Honey leaned down, picking the star up. She touched the sticky goo, watching as it dripped from her fingers. *"Honey?"* The calico turned her head to the outskirts, from which the star had been thrown.

Velcro turned back to the beehive, watching her rear to make sure that Honey followed. Once there, she bolted into the trees, hiding within the forest's shadows. She looked down, watching as Honey rolled up to the beehive.

"Velcro?" Honey whispered, looking around frantically. "Is that you, Velcro?"

"You haven't sent word in some time," Velcro spoke from the trees.

Honey looked up, squinting her eyes as she searched above for her friend. "Sweety, this is way too dangerous. You shouldn't be here. And neither should I, for that matter."

"I need an update," Velcro said firmly. "I haven't heard from you in a while. What is the Devil Corps planning? Are they falling back on their attacks? Are they regrouping? What's the deal?"

"We really shouldn't be having this conversation right here."

"We're safe," Velcro assured her, "I've already scouted the area. We're completely isolated."

"I don't know, sweety," Honey shook her head. "I just, I... I don't feel right talking about that stuff here."

Velcro lifted an eyebrow. "What's the deal, Honey? You've stopped sending word, and now that I'm here, you still won't say anything. What aren't you telling me?"

Honey pulled her head away, turning towards the ground. "It's... it's complicated."

"Nothing's too complicated for you," Velcro snapped back. "Lets hear it."

Honey took in a deep breath. "It's, well..." She lifted her head, staring back into the trees at her friend. "They know there's a leak, Velcro. How else could someone be ambushing every single attack squad? They're becoming suspicious, and let's face it, I'm the new gal on the Counsel, so I'm the number one suspect."

"So then you're going to just stop giving me intel," Velcro glared, "just because they're aware of a leak?"

"What other choice do I have, Velcro?"

"You don't have any other choice," Velcro replied. "Without that intel, I wouldn't have been able to save all of those villages. And without any further intel, *who knows* what other villages are feeling the wrath of the Devil Corps. Oh wait, that's right, *you* know!"

Honey cringed. "It's not that simple-"

"But it is," Velcro cut her off. "It is that simple. People might be dying out there right now. And I could be there to stop it, but I can't do that if you're holding that information back."

"Velcro," Honey raised her voice, "they'll kill me if I keep doing it."

"And *thousands* will die if you *don't*."

Honey bit her tongue. She turned her head away, sadness in her eyes.

Velcro let out a sigh. "Honey," she spoke in a calmer voice. "I can't do this without you. We're at war now. And I need to know whose side you're on."

"I..." Honey's jaw began to tremble. "I'm sorry," she said in a pitiful voice. "I can't."

"Then I can no longer trust you." Velcro hopped down from the tree. Standing behind Honey, she unsheathed her sword. As she stared at the calico from behind, she couldn't help but gulp as she pointed the blade to Honey's neck.

"Wait," Honey said. "I have one last thing to tell you," she spoke through tear filled eyes. "Then after that, you can do whatever it is you want to do, sweety."

Velcro raised her blade away, motioning for her to go on.

"It's about your home village, Highland. It's on the latest list to be attacked."

'*What?!*' Velcro's eyes bulged at the announcement.

"I was actually going to send you that last bit of intel," Honey confessed, "but that would've been the last you'd hear from me."

Velcro sheathed her sword, turning her back to the calico.

"So you're gonna just let me go," Honey asked, looking over her shoulder, "even though I'm the enemy now?"

"Honey," Velcro spoke sternly. "You're so much better than this. We could really use someone like you on our side in this fight. I wish you wouldn't walk down this path."

"Girl," Honey smirked, sniffing her snotty nose. "I don't know if you noticed, but I can't walk *at all* anymore. And until I can, I really don't know how much help I'd actually be."

"Until you can?" Velcro glanced back curiously.

"Oh nothing." Honey turned her head down. "Just wishful thinking from a young, crippled Devil."

Velcro furrowed her eyebrows. She didn't know what to make of her old friend, but she knew that she couldn't trust her anymore. '*But even so,*' Velcro thought, '*There's no time to waste. I have no choice but to trust she's telling the truth about Highland.*' So without even a farewell, Velcro zipped away into the night, leaving her friend behind one last time.

Chapter 31

"That was the last time I heard from her," Velcro told Maggie. "I returned to Highland. And sure enough, I ran into a small squad of Devils, heading right for the village. It was the first time I'd been home in years, so I figured I'd stick around, to make sure everything was okay.

"But then Charlie had the bright idea to dress up his lackeys as Devils and lure me out." Velcro shook her head. "Stupid me, I fell right for the bait. That was the first I've seen my brother in years." She chuckled, rolling her eyes. "And after all this time, he's still an idiot."

"Mm," Maggie made another sound. "Mm-hm. It doesn't sound much to me like you get along very well with your brother."

"Heh, ya think?" Velcro smirked, but as she changed the subject, her smile disappeared. "But it was just after my brief scuffle with him that I met with the hamsters. They confirmed my worst fears, that the Devils had succeeded in one of their attacks, and I wasn't there to stop it.

"They recruited me for a rescue mission. I saw this as my chance to finally put a real dent in the Devil Corps' plans. And after what I discovered within the walls of this prison, I thought I finally found my ticket to ending this war once and for all. But look how that turned out. I came here originally to try and rescue the hamsters held prisoner. Now I'm the one who needs rescuing. I'm the one being held prisoner."

"Mm. That's too bad, child," Maggie said.

"Yeah," Velcro sighed.

"Let me tell you," Maggie started, "when you get out of here-"

"*If* I get out of here," Velcro corrected.

"Now now, don't be thinkin' that way, child. When you *do* get out of here, I'd love it if you could do something for me."

"Huh?" Velcro's ears perked up. "What's that?"

"Go home," Maggie said, "and ask your brother for his help."

"What?" Velcro scowled, raising a curious eyebrow. "Why do you keep bringing him up?"

"Because, child, he's all the family you have left." There was sorrow in Maggie's words. "And it pains me to hear you speak so ill of him. You've pushed him so far away during a time when you need each other the most."

Velcro's scowl faded away as her eyebrows rose.

"When you get out of here," Maggie continued, "I want you to at least try to make amends with him. You're both still so young, and I'd hate for you to get to be my age and look back with regrets. Lord I wish I could've handled things differently with my own little sis. But sadly, I don't have that chance to go back and make things right with her anymore."

Velcro pulled her head to her side. Her eyes dipped down as she pondered over Maggie's words. "I," she hesitated. "I don't know."

"What's not to know?" Maggie asked.

Velcro didn't respond, however. '*I never even thought about that, and even after she told me what happened with her*

141

sister.' Velcro smacked her palm to her forehead. *'Tsk, I probably sound like a self-centered little brat. What was I thinking?'*

Maggie broke the silence. "Of course you're free to do as you like. Don't let a tired old hag like me tell you how to live your life, child."

"No, it's not that," Velcro said. "It's just..."

"I didn't mean to lecture you," Maggie quickly added. "Now go ahead, child. Let me hear, what happens next in this tale of yours?"

"What do you mean?" Velcro asked. "That's it. I got caught, locked away, and now I'm sitting in a cell, talking to you. And that's as far as it goes."

"Yes," Maggie said, "but what happens *next?*"

"What are you talking about?"

"I mean, how are you going to get out? After all, this can't be it, can it? This can't really be the way the Tale of the Ninja Kat ends."

Velcro lifted her head. She had a sincere look on her face as she stared over towards the dalmatian's cell. "Maggie-"

KABOOM!

An ear-splitting explosion cut the prisoners' conversation short. Velcro sprang to her feet, rushing to the door of her cell. Grabbing hold of the bars, she peered to the far end of the hallway, which was covered in a mask of smoke. "What in the world?!"

Chapter 32

Velcro peered out through the bars of her cell, watching as the smoke from the explosion cleared up. *'What in the world is going on out there?'*

She heard a faint buzzing among the sounds of crumpling debris. *'Wait, is that-?'* A bee zipped out from the smoke, flying right up to Velcro's nose. Velcro stared down at the familiar bee with perplexed eyes. "Buzzbee?"

"*YEEEE-HAAAAWWWW!*"

Velcro snapped back to the hole, watching with widened eyes as Buttons skidded into the hallway within his ball. "Buttons? But how?" Buttons was followed by Chippy, who was carrying the Boogie Man on his head. Velcro cautiously eyed the small rabbit. *'Could it have been him?'*

Buttons ran over to Velcro's cell. He paused, staring up at the cat with a look of confusion. He leaned forward, sniffing out at the brown tabby.

"Uh..." Velcro raised a brow.

"Gadzooks, it is you!" Buttons sprang back with a wide eyed grin. "Wowee, now whoda thunk that that there Ninja Kat was really a girl this whole time?"

Velcro's brow continued to flicker. "Come again?"

"No time to waste," Buttons cut her short, "we've got to get you and the rest of the hams outta here."

He grabbed hold of the bars to Velcro's cell. "Ngh!" He tried with all his might to pry them open, straining himself in the process. "It's no use. Chip, come on over here and gimme a hand, will ya?"

Just then, the bars to all of the cells automatically slid open. "Huh?" Buttons looked over to see that Chippy had pulled a lever at the end of the hall. "Er, uh, good work, Chip! That was gonna be my next plan!" Chippy just tilted his head in response, feigning a smile at his little friend.

"Let's go," Buttons motioned Velcro, "we already got the rest of the hams out, you're our last stop."

"You already released the other hamsters?" Velcro shook her head. "But how did you-?"

"No time to explain." Buttons pointed to the lop-eared rabbit sitting on Chippy's head. "The little guy says we gotta go, so we gotta go." Buttons and Chippy ran back to the hole, with Buzzbee trailing behind them.

Velcro started to follow, but stopped after a few steps. She turned back, rushing to Maggie's cell. She stood at the entrance, seeing the old dalmatian for the first time.

Maggie was covered in rags. She looked up at Velcro with her tired eyes, sitting on the foot of her bed with her hands in her lap. "You go on without me, child." Maggie forced a smile on her aged face. "My place is here."

"What are you talking about?" Velcro huffed. "I'm not leaving you here."

"I'm just an old pup, Velcro," Maggie shrugged her shoulders. "And besides, after what I did, I deserve to be here."

Velcro pursed her mouth. "That's a lie and you know it."

"Hmm?"

"You told me yourself that you've thought about

144

leaving this place." Velcro motioned towards the hole with a swipe. "Well, now's your chance, so don't just sit there and pretend like you belong here."

"Child-"

"Don't you 'child' me," Velcro snapped. "You want to make up for what happened with your sister? Well, rotting away in a cell isn't going to help matters at all."

Maggie's eyes were suddenly awake. Her jaw began to drop as she stared in amazement at the ranting cat.

"You said that all of this started with Molly. Well, if you want to make up for what happened to her, then get out of this damn prison and help me put an end to this war."

"Hey there," Buttons yelled back, "we ain't got time for chattin', we've gotta get a move on."

Maggie hadn't budged as she looked up in awe at the brown tabby. "Velcro-"

The cat snatched Maggie by the wrist. "Let's go!"

Velcro dragged the old dog to her feet. She tugged her out of her cell, pulling her all the way to the end of the hall.

"W-wait a minute, child," Maggie stammered.

"No time." Velcro caught up with Buttons, who waited behind for her. "Where's Chippy?"

"He's already leading the other hams out," Buttons said, as Buzzbee swirled around his head. "Now come on, Buzzbee will show us the way."

"Alright," Velcro nodded.

"Now wait just one minute," Maggie demanded, tugging her arm away from Velcro. She stood up straight, rubbing her wrist.

Velcro sighed. "*Maggie,*" she said in an almost pleading tone.

"No, Velcro." Maggie shook her head. "If I'm to

escape from this prison-" She paused, looking at the cat with a serious glare. She struggled to keep a straight face, however, as her smile proved too overpowering. "If I'm to finally leave this place, then the least that I can do is walk out on my own with some dignity."

Velcro smirked. "Now that's more like it."

"Great," Buttons exasperated. "Now can we finally *get out of here?*"

Buzzbee lead the way to the exit. As they fled from the building, the sun shining down blinded the party. Velcro rose her arm to block the sun, squinting as her vision slowly recovered.

They were greeted by a hoard of newly released hamsters standing within the prison grounds. They were all standing still, as if they were frozen in place. "What's going on," Velcro questioned, "why aren't we moving?"

Velcro pushed her way through the group, Maggie and Buttons following behind. Velcro saw Chippy up ahead, with the Boogie Man cowering down behind his head. "No," Velcro muttered under her breath, shoving her way to the front.

She gulped. Her eyes widened, and a single bead of sweat dripped down her face.

"Ahhh, you made it, yes."

The Spider stood before them. And behind him, a legion of Devils and mindless, mechanized creatures were rearing for a slaughter.

146

Chapter 33

Velcro outstretched her arms, holding back the group of hamster. She stood her ground, glaring at the menacing army before her. *'Crap. Now what?'*

"Just in time for the main event, yes," the Spider chuckled.

"Buttons," Velcro growled through her teeth. "You lead the hamsters out of here. Chippy, I'm gonna need you to help hold these guys back."

"Are you crazy?" Buttons asked. "How do you expect to hold them all back all on your own?"

"I don't know," Velcro dipped her head. She took in a deep breath. Then she snapped her gaze forward, staring down the Spider with fire in her eyes. "But that doesn't matter. What matters is getting everybody out alive. So don't worry about me. You just worry about getting all of these hamsters out of here."

Velcro turned to Chippy. "You ready, big guy?"

Chippy tilted his doe eyed head. He shook away his doubts, then nodded. He pressed a fist to his chest, then smiled with confidence back at the cat.

Then the Boogie Man jumped off Chippy's head. As he hopped forward, the cat looked down curiously at him. "What are you doing?"

"You go," the Boogie Man spoke. "I stay. I change into big meanie. I fight big mean Spider man."

"No way," Velcro said, "you can't take them all on by yourself."

"You're right," Maggie concurred, placing a palm on Velcro's shoulder. "And so, I'll stay behind with him and help hold them off."

"Not you, too," Velcro snapped at Maggie. "You'll just get yourself killed."

"Heh, you think so?" Maggie smirked. "Well, you may be right. But I'll have you know that I was the strongest fighter in my day. And while I may be old now, I'm not nearly as out of shape as I look, child."

Maggie pulled Velcro behind her, taking a fighting stance.

"Do you really think I'm gonna just stand by and let you do this?" Velcro asked.

"No, you were right before. Rotting away in a prison cell, that wasn't doing anything to make up for what happened with my little sis." Maggie turned to face Velcro. "I'm just a tired old pup. There's little I can do to help in this war at my age. But you're too important to lose now. What the people need is for you to go on. Start by saving these hamsters. And lead the resistance against the Devil Corps."

"Maggie-"

"I'm not taking no for an answer, child." Maggie turned back to the opposition.

Velcro gaped at Maggie. She looked back at the hoard of frightened hamsters behind her. Then she nodded her head with a sigh. "Okay," she said. "I got it."

"I hate to interrupt this touching moment," the Spider chimed in. "But I'm beginning to grow quite bored waiting around for you to decide whether or not you want to vainly attempt to escape my Web."

The Boogie Man growled. "You all leave now." He already began to shake, and his body began to slowly expand.

"Oh?" The Spider was intrigued by the brown rabbit. "Oh my, now this is interesting, yes."

"Oh crap," Buttons yelped. "We gotta get outta here. Once he's changed, he won't be able to tell the difference between us and them."

"Alright," Velcro turned to Buttons and Chippy. "You two lead the way. I'll watch the rear."

"Got it," Buttons said, raising his arm in the air. "All right everyone, lets get on outta here!"

Buttons lead the pack as they headed towards the outskirts. The path was clear, and the Spider didn't even seem interested in stopping them. His attention remained preoccupied.

The hamsters managed to make it mere feet away from the fencing. But then the enemy cut them off. Buttons and Chippy skidded to a halt. The two hams stared at their foes with fear, which quickly evolved into confusion. Then as they took in a whiff of their enemies' scent, the hamsters' eyes widened in unison.

Meanwhile, Velcro watched as the hamsters stepped off. She turned to Maggie one last time before joining them. "You be careful, Maggie."

"Don't you worry about me, child." Maggie responded.

"Maggie..." Velcro paused, as the last of the hamsters ran past her.

"And one more thing," Maggie looked back with a smile. "Thank you, Velcro."

Velcro tailed the hamsters, watching out for the

Spider's legion. Immediately, several Devils charged towards the pack.

Maggie rushed to the pursuers. "I don't think so." One of the Devils swung a bo at her. She caught it under her arm, swinging a fist with the other. Taking the bo as her prize, she used it to fight off the remaining pursuers.

As Velcro looked back on this action, the Boogie Man grabbed her attention. He turned to the air, letting out a yowl as he grew to great heights. She witnessed the rabbit's transformation. His limbs became long and limber. His nose sprouted out, resembling a wolf's snout, and his long ears hang back behind his head. He stretched out his claws, roaring out a war cry at the Spider and his minions.

The very sight of the monstrous rabbit sent chills through Velcro's body. She was so distracted that she ran into the hamsters in front of her, not realizing that they had stopped again.

"What the... *Now* what?" Velcro rushed through the pack, making it back to the front. They had been cut off again. And as she saw who had blocked them off, her reaction mirrored that of the hamsters'. This time, blocking their path was the brother duo of Flash and Slash.

Buttons muttered from his gaping mouth, "Flash?"

They didn't have another moment to react before their reunion was cut short. The Boogie Man crashed down in front of the group. He let out a deafening roar, one which made even the robotic hamsters take a step back.

The monstrous Boogie Man stepped towards Flash and Slash. They attempted to double team the monster, but it was futile. He clasped a single hand around each of the hamsters. As they struggled within his grasp, the Boogie Man howled once more into the air before flinging them effortlessly to the Spider's legion.

150

'How in the world?' Velcro was stunned by the Boogie Man's new strength.

With the opposition out of the way, all that stood in Velcro and the hamster's way was the towering Boogie Man. He looked over his shoulder, glaring down at Velcro with malice in his eye. The group collectively gulped, as they leaned backwards away from from the monster.

"Get out," he growled, the last of his normally timid self shimmering through for just a moment.

Velcro's body shivered. She blinked several times before realizing that he posed no threat. Yet.

"Right," Velcro turned to the hamsters. "This way." She lead them around the brewing battlefield. "Buttons-"

"On it!" He rolled up into his ball, crashing through the fencing and creating a hole in which to escape from. Velcro stood to the side, watching to make sure everyone made it safely through the fence.

After the last of the hamsters made it through, she began to follow after. But she stopped. She turned to face the battle scene one last time. The Boogie Man had rejoined the fight, tossing the mechanized critters around like rag dolls.

And Maggie was doing surprisingly well herself, fighting defensively and holding back as many of the Devils as her aged body could handle. The Spider, however, was nowhere to be found on the field.

Velcro couldn't help but feel uneasy as she observed the battle from afar. She hated leaving her comrades behind to fight for her. But she knew that she couldn't stay. Not in this battle. She had a bigger role to play later on.

Chapter 34

Back at the hamster's hideout, a light celebration was under way. All of the hamsters were catching up and joking around, relieved to have finally escaped. Chippy was munching away on Thomasina's treats, while Buttons was getting a kick showing off his new gadgets to the younger hams.

While everyone was having a good time, Velcro kept to herself. She sat alone in a chair, leaning forward with fists under her chin. She was once again lost in thought.

A paw landed on Velcro's shoulder, pulling her back to reality. Velcro looked up to find Huck, who smiled back at the cat. "Ah, don't look so down. You did well."

"I did well?" Velcro asked. "What exactly did I *do*? You all had to come to *my* rescue."

"True," Huck agreed. "But, it was your guidance that lead us into the enemy's territory. And it was your motivation that drove us to complete the mission, even after you had been captured. Without your help, we would have never even made it inside The Web in the first place, let alone free all of these hamsters."

"But what about the rest of them?" Velcro argued. "What about Flash? And all the others being used by the Spider?"

Huck nodded. "Ah, well, we just have to take our victories one at a time. For now, we were able to free everyone here, which is a victory all it's own. And the next step will be to free all those who remain under the Spider's control."

Velcro considered the Elder Ham's words, but she ultimately shook her head in disagreement. "No, that's not the next step."

"Hmm? Then what is?"

"Those guys are strong." Velcro looked away from Huck, staring out into space. "They're way stronger than any of us. It's that Magic, that Black Magic that they're using. After seeing what it did to that rabbit, I know that we don't stand a chance against them in our current condition."

Huck brushed a paw through his mustache. "What are you suggesting?"

Velcro turned back to the Elder Ham. "Are you sure that you told me everything that you know about Magic?"

"Oh yes, I'm quite positive. But just what are you getting at exactly?"

"Huck, I need to learn how to use Magic myself."

"Hmm, I see."

Velcro raised a brow. "What, no objections? Considering how reluctant you were at first-"

"No no, I still don't approve. However," Huck sighed, "after all that's transpired, I can see how you've come to this conclusion." Huck brought his paw down to his chin, nodding his head as he stared at the floor.

"Very well," he concluded. "I've heard rumors of a Magician from the village of Redfield. Do you know where that is?"

"Yes," Velcro responded. "I've heard of it."

"Good. This Magician's name is Shiki. She was

recently banished from Redfield for her use of Magic, though it's possible that some within the village may yet know where she resides."

"Shiki, huh?"

"Yes," the Elder Ham confirmed. "Go to Redfield. Find Shiki. Then, even if you can't wield Magic yourself, then perhaps you'll at least discover a weakness that we can use against the Devil Corps' use of Black Magic."

"Wait," Velcro paused the hamster, "why wouldn't I be able to use Magic?"

"It's as I told you before. Not everyone can wield Magic. But who knows?" Huck shrugged his shoulders. "Maybe you're not a *bad egg* after all."

Velcro scrunched up her eyebrows. *'Bad egg?'*

Huck lifted his paw to the ceiling. "Here." He made a gesture, summoning a single bee down from above. "Take Buzzbee with you." The bee flew right past the elder. It swirled around the cat's head, as she followed it with her eyes intensely. "I think you'll find him to be of some assistance on your journey."

Velcro held out her palm, and Buzzbee landed on it. The bee looked right at Velcro, lifting one of its tiny little limbs to a buzzing salute. Velcro couldn't help but let out a chuckle.

"Ah, and before I forget," Huck scrambled away, yelling out for Thomasina. He found her as she was setting out more treats for the partying hamsters. Chippy was rubbing his hands together in anticipation.

"Ah, there you are, Thomasina," Huck said, shooing Chippy out of the way. "Could you be so kind as to fetch our friend's new garments?"

"Oh certainly!" Thomasina said, running off with her treats still in hand. Huck smiled back at Velcro, while Chippy

154

frowned and dipped his head.

Thomasina ran back with a set of folded clothes in her arms. "Here you are," she said, handing them over to Velcro. Buzzbee flew out of the cat's hand as she accepted the clothing.

Huck placed an arm over Thomasina's shoulder. "After seeing how torn up your old outfit kept getting, I had Thomasina knit you a new one."

"I sure hope you like it," Thomasina said, clasping her hands together.

"You can try them on in the other room," Huck pointed across the room with his cane. "Go ahead now."

Velcro smiled, then headed to the room. It was much quieter with the noise from the party muffled out. She walked in front of a mirror. She looked down at the clothes in her arms, then lifted her head to stare at her own reflection.

'It was all I could do to leave them behind again,' Velcro thought. *'Flash. And the rabbit. And-'*

"Go home," Maggie's voice spoke in her head, *"ask your brother for his help."*

Velcro's eyes shifted. *'Wait a minute, why did I just think that?'*

"Because he's all the family you have left. You've pushed him so far away during a time when you need each other the most."

Velcro looked away from the mirror. Letting out a huff, she shook her head. *'Charlie...'*

Knock! Knock!

"What do you think, dear?" Thomasina spoke through the door. "Do you like it?"

"Uh," Velcro looked back down at her clothes, then snapped her head to the door. "Just a minute."

Velcro slipped on the new outfit. "Huh," Velcro said, admiring at herself in the mirror. Like her old one, it was black all over, and made for a tight, sleek fit. Her top was now sleeveless, and it had a slight v-neck, revealing a portion of the fishnet style armor that she wore underneath. She twisted her body, seeing how she looked from all angles.

"Heh," she smirked, placing her fists on her hips. "I like it."

To be continued in Velcro: The Green Lion

Chris Widdop grew up with his cat, Velcro. And together, the two would constantly escape into the fantasy world that was their vivid imaginations, where they took part in many adventures. Now, as a young, new writer, Chris wants nothing more than to share those adventures with the world.

He also reputably likes chicken. Chicken is delicious.